She dreamt of him that night.

Not of Brian, but of her late husband. The dream was so real, so frightening she could feel herself breaking out into a cold sweat. It was only after a few moments had passed that she realized there was no one standing over her, that the heavy breathing she heard was her own.

Still, she couldn't shake the feeling that someone had been in the room with her.

Turning on the lamp beside her bed didn't reveal anyone standing in the shadows, or taking shelter behind her drapes.

She was alone.

And maybe going a little crazy.

Lila took a long breath, trying to steady her nerves. She was about to turn off the light again when the phone rang. Lila yanked the receiver. "Look, you sick, perverted scum, you keep this up and I'm going to track you down and trust me, you *really* don't want me to do that."

"Oh, I don't know, it sounds promising," the deep male voice on the other end said.

Lila was stunned. And relieved. He was the man she *wanted* to hear from. "Brian…"

Dear Reader,

Yes, I know. I said the past Cavanaugh book would be the last Cavanaugh book. I lied. This is a result of all those nice letters and e-mails I received, asking for Brian to have his own story (Brian thanks you). I must confess, I did miss them. After spending so much time with the Cavanaughs, they have become almost real for me. In this book, Brian is reunited with his ex-partner, Lila McIntyre. They have a very special bond inasmuch as he once saved her life. And, truth be told, there was a lot of electricity going on inside the police vehicle they shared for six years. Neither one acted on it because at the time they were married to other people. Now, both single, Lila and Brian are paired up when she finds herself on the receiving end of mysterious phone calls in the middle of the night. Brian is more than happy to come to the rescue. And thereby hangs a tale.

As always, I thank you for reading and I wish you much love in your life.

Love,

Marie Ferrarella

MARIE FERRARELLA

Cavanaugh Heat

Romantic
SUSPENSE

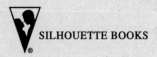 SILHOUETTE BOOKS

ISBN-13: 978-0-373-27569-4
ISBN-10:   0-373-27569-2

CAVANAUGH HEAT

Copyright © 2008 by Marie Rydzynski-Ferrarella

All rights reserved. Except for use in any review, the reproduction
or utilization of this work in whole or in part in any form by any
electronic, mechanical or other means, now known or hereafter
invented, including xerography, photocopying and recording, or in
any information storage or retrieval system, is forbidden without
the written permission of the editorial office, Silhouette Books,
233 Broadway, New York, NY 10279 U.S.A.

This is a work of fiction. Names, characters, places and incidents are
either the product of the author's imagination or are used fictitiously, and
any resemblance to actual persons, living or dead, business establishments,
events or locales is entirely coincidental.

This edition published by arrangement with Harlequin Books S.A.

® and TM are trademarks of Harlequin Books S.A., used under license.
Trademarks indicated with ® are registered in the United States Patent
and Trademark Office, the Canadian Trade Marks Office and in other
countries.

Visit Silhouette Books at www.eHarlequin.com

Printed in U.S.A.

Books by Marie Ferrarella

Silhouette Romantic Suspense

In Broad Daylight #1315
Alone in the Dark #1327
Dangerous Disguise #1339
The Heart of a Ruler #1412
The Woman Who Wasn't There #1415
Cavanaugh Watch #1431
Her Lawman on Call #1451
Diagnosis: Danger #1460
My Spy #1472
Her Sworn Protector #1491
Cavanaugh Heat #1499

Silhouette Special Edition

Her Good Fortune #1665
Because a Husband is Forever #1671
The Measure of a Man #1706
She's Having a Baby #1713
Her Special Charm #1726
Husbands and Other Strangers #1736
The Prodigal M.D. Returns #1775
Mother in Training #1785
Remodeling the Bachelor #1845
Taming the Playboy #1856
Capturing the Millionaire #1863
Falling for the M.D. #1873

MARIE FERRARELLA

This *USA TODAY* bestselling and RITA® Award-winning author has written over 150 novels for Silhouette Books, some under the name Marie Nicole. Her romances are beloved by fans worldwide.

To Audrey, who gives me unconditional love and a reason to vacuum every day.

Chapter 1

The abrupt ring of the telephone didn't wake her.

Despite the fact that she'd gone to bed more than an hour ago, she was still awake. Tense.

Waiting.

Waiting to have the last fragments of serenity wrenched from her. Again. It had been happening more and more frequently. The middle-of-the-night phone calls shattering her peace of mind.

She supposed that she could have closed off the landline, muting the ringer so that when the call came, it wouldn't register, wouldn't cause her heart to race.

But she couldn't shut the phone. She didn't have that luxury because if one of her children called, if she shut off the phone, she wouldn't be able to take the call. She didn't want to worry them, making them wonder why she wasn't home at this hour or wasn't answering her phone.

Or they could need her. All four of them, Zack, Taylor, Riley and even Frank, were on the force as she had been.

As their late father had been.

She would never be able to forgive herself if she missed a life-and-death call just because some phantom nutcase seemed bent on spooking her.

Sitting up, Lila McIntyre turned on the lamp and squinted at the light's harsh intrusion. Over in the corner, Duchess, her ten-year-old German shepherd, picked up her head as if to ask, "What's wrong?"

"Go back to sleep," she told the dog, but Duchess kept on eyeing the ringing phone. And wouldn't stop until she answered it.

Edgy, Lila felt like throwing the phone across the room instead of picking up the receiver. With effort, she made herself calm down. Whoever was on the other end of the line wanted her to lose control. If she gave in to a fit of temper, she'd be playing into his hands, doing exactly what he wanted her to do.

Lila looked at the phone's LCD screen. All it told her was that the incoming call was "out-of-area." No number, no hint.

Whoever it was was playing mind games, she thought. But why? Nothing came to her.

Maybe it was just a nut job, pure and simple. It was the most plausible explanation, but her intuition told her no.

Drawing in a long breath, Lila snatched up the receiver and pressed it to her ear. The very act made her shiver.

"Hello?" she snapped. It wasn't a greeting, but a demand. A demand for a reply.

There was no answer on the other end of the line. Only the faint sound of someone breathing. Someone listening to the sound of her voice while keeping his own a secret.

What do you want from me? she asked silently.

Out loud, she did her best to sound bored. "You know, this isn't funny anymore. I can have this traced and when I find out who you are, there are going to be consequences. Consequences you're not going to like." Lila looked down and saw that she had dug her nails into the comforter, gathering it into a wad. She released it—but wasn't able to do the same with the tension that rode roughshod over her. "So why don't you do yourself a favor and stop acting like an eight-year-old?"

There was no response, just another soft breath drawn in and exhaled. And then came a "click" in her ear. The caller was gone.

Lila sat there, holding the receiver, annoyed with herself. Annoyed because she was allowing this jerk to get to her.

"If you'd like to place a call…"

Lila jumped as the metallic female voice instructed her to dial again. With a muffled curse, she threw the receiver into the cradle. The recording was abruptly silenced.

Her hand shook as she dragged it through tousled honey-blond hair.

It was the twenty-first call.

By definition, a peace officer should like peace. Despite the fact that he had risen up through the ranks and was now the chief of detectives, a position he had held for quite some time, Brian Cavanaugh still considered himself a peace officer.

A peace officer who hated peace and quiet.

Oh, he didn't hate it on the streets of Aurora, a city that he and rather a large portion of his family patrolled and thought of as their own. The peace on the streets was something he took exceptional pride in. Maintaining it was what he was all about—professionally. The peace and quiet he hated was the type that assaulted him when he first opened his eyes in the morning. The kind that slapped him across the face when he walked through the front door of his house every evening.

Not all that long ago, that same house rang with the sounds of voices, as likely as not raised either in laughter or in frustrated fits of temper that dissolved as quickly as they materialized. The voices of his wife and his children, three boys and a girl.

An amused smile curved his mouth. He could just hear their response to that. They wouldn't have taken kindly to being referred to as children. They saw themselves as—and were—adults. Three men and a woman—all of whom would always be his children long after they traded in their service revolvers and law books for canes.

Troy, Jared, Dax and Janelle were all married now and Susan, his wife, had died by her own hand several years ago. Leaving him with a whole lot of empty space. What had once been a home had become a house where he laundered his clothes, slept and, on occasion, ate.

Most of the time, though, he took his meals either at his desk or at Andrew's, his older brother's house. Andrew was a veritable Houdini when it came to pulling food out of the air. No matter how many faces popped up at the extended table that Andrew had had specially made, a table that could sit twenty-six, Andrew always seemed to have enough food to feed everyone. And there was always enough left over for seconds and possibly thirds.

Andrew's hospitality was legendary and family was all important to him.

It was all important to all of them, Brian thought now as he closed a folder on his desk. He'd just never realized how much it meant to him until he'd walked down the aisle and given Janelle away, then returned home after the reception.

And woken up the following morning to absolutely nothing. No noise, no sounds of a door being opened and shut, nothing. Nothing but all-enshrouding peace and quiet.

And damn, but he hated it.

"Don't you ever go home anymore?"

The soft query caught him off guard. He hadn't been looking toward the entrance to his office. Instead his attention had been fixed on the portal that led him to the past. Remembering times when his life was so full he hadn't had two seconds to rub together. That was when his kids were younger, all still living at home, and Susan—well, there was no getting away from it. Susan had been waning, even then.

It had been a draining juggling act, working on the force and standing guard on the home front, making sure that no one suspected the deep bouts of depression that Susan battled. He thought it would be detrimental for his children to know the depths to which their mother could sink. He was fairly certain he was successful in his efforts, that no one suspected how bad Susan was.

No one except for him and Andrew, who always seemed to know everything. And, of course, Susan, who, when she managed to rise above the leaden blanket that would eventually smother her, would look at him with those brown eyes of hers and silently ask, "Why?"

He had no answer. No one did. No one knew why she would periodically drift away mentally. Her returns grew fewer and fewer as well as shorter and shorter. Until one day she was gone altogether, body and mind. That was the day she committed suicide, leaving a note that said she was sorry, but she couldn't help herself.

It was a sense of family that kept him going then. That and his duty to the city where he and his brothers, and then his children, nieces and nephews were born. The city that they now served.

Seeing the slim, blond-haired woman in the doorway took him back, as well. Back to the days when he was a homicide detective. And Lila McIntyre was his partner.

"Damn best partner anyone had ever had," he'd told her more than once.

And he'd meant it.

A multitude of emotions tangoed through his mind, dominated by the almost sickening fear he'd felt that night he'd had Lila's blood seeping through the spaces between his fingers as he pressed down for all he was worth on the hole a bullet had torn in her side.

"Nothing to go home for anymore," he answered simply. Brian placed the folder in his top drawer, then shut it. "My family's grown and off making families of their own. Just the four walls and me now."

Lila came a little closer, smiling that smile he'd once been able to read so well. The bittersweet one that used to make him ache inside for reasons he would never allow himself to dwell on.

"You need a dog," she told him. "Duchess was a great help after…" Her voice trailed off, the smile intensified. "After," Lila repeated with a sigh, making no effort to finish the thought.

They both knew what she was not saying. After Ben

had been killed. That had been over three years ago. Ben McIntyre had been another detective on the force. Unlike either of them, he had worked in the vice squad. Ben had been a victim of a drug bust gone bad or his own greed, depending on who you spoke to.

It was the latter theory that had been shadowing Lila and her four children these last few years. Causing them grief. But Ben was gone either way and she had managed to soldier on, continuing to work at the precinct, her head always held high.

He'd always thought of her as a magnificent woman.

He'd always thought of her, even when he shouldn't have.

Brian looked at her now, thinking that Lila bore no visible scars of what she'd gone through. She still looked exactly like the young woman he'd been paired up with almost fourteen years ago. He couldn't help comparing her to Susan, to how differently the two women bore up to things.

Lila's life had been hard—few thought she would survive the wound that took her away from active duty—and yet here she was, still young and vibrant. In comparison, Susan had had almost everything she wanted and yet somehow that had never been enough. His wife had allowed life to leave ravaging marks on her until she finally just faded from existence.

Not fair, he upbraided himself. *Susan was your wife, where's your loyalty?*

He had no answer to his own silent question. What

he did have was a fair amount of guilt for even allowing his thoughts to succumb to this contest of mentally weighing and measuring between the two women.

There was no point to this. The past was gone and nothing could ever change that.

Brian focused his attention on the here and now. On the woman standing near his desk. Everyone else from the day shift had long since gone home. The Lila he remembered never did anything without a reason. Their paths, whether by design or by happenstance, hadn't crossed for a long time. Why now? What was she doing here when by all rights she should have been home?

"So what brings you here?" Brian asked, doing his best to bank down the awkwardness that came from losing touch with an old friend.

"Same old Brian." Her smile lost some of its bittersweetness, replaced by a broad ribbon of amusement. "Nice to know that some things don't change. You always did get right to the point."

He laughed. He'd never been very good at small talk. As he recalled, neither had she. "Must have been the company I kept." He looked at her for a long moment. Something was bothering her. Did it have to do with one of her kids? "You were never known for beating around the bush, either."

Lila inclined her head, honey-blond bangs falling into her blue eyes. She moved them impatiently out of the way.

"Touché." She glanced at the chair that stood before his desk and nodded toward it. "May I sit?"

He gestured for her to do just that. "You don't have to ask. We *are* friends, remember?"

In a fluid motion, Lila slid onto the chair. Her figure was still fighting trim even though she spent her days behind a desk now. From a distance, she could have been mistaken for one of her daughters. All four of the McIntyre offspring were here, on the force, all bravely ignoring the hail of insinuations and slurs regarding their father's character until it had finally run its course.

Though he'd never really liked Ben McIntyre, he had come to the man's posthumous defense. There was not enough proof to convict Ben or Dean Walker, his dead partner, of the whispered accusations. Brian was a firm believer in the "innocent until proven guilty" aspect of the law no matter what his personal feelings might be. Shortly before Ben's death, the man had accused him of sleeping with Lila.

Susan had voiced the same accusations, but in Susan's case, her insecurities and demons put words into her mouth. In Ben's case, it was just unfounded jealousy. Even so, Brian wouldn't allow that to dictate his feelings about Ben's complicity in the missing drug money. Just because Ben was a poor excuse for a human being didn't mean he was a dirty cop, as well. And thus far, there wasn't enough evidence to convict him or absolve him.

"Yes, we are," Lila was saying. "Friends."

Banking down a sigh, Lila raised her eyes to his. She had no idea where to start, how to phrase this without sounding like some old woman who habitually checked beneath her bed each night for intruders before going to sleep.

She knotted her fingers together in her lap, searching for the right words.

Brian frowned slightly. Her body language spoke of feelings that seemed the total antithesis of the woman he'd once known. Known her as well as he'd known himself.

"Are you nervous, Lila?"

Even as he asked, it seemed impossible. One of the first things he'd ever taken her to task for was that she didn't have the good sense to be afraid. She was fearless—and this tended to get rookies commendations…and killed.

Denial instantly sprang to Lila's lips. But this wasn't something to lie about. Especially not to Brian. Not to her old partner.

She looked down at her knotted hands, then raised her eyes to his again.

"Yes," she answered, her voice so soft it almost disappeared into the atmosphere without leaving behind a sound.

Concerned, he leaned forward, the very movement creating an intimate space between them. For more than six years, they had had each other's backs, gone into dangerous situations without knowing if either one of them would make it back alive. There was a time when there was no one he trusted more than Lila. They'd been so in-tuned to one another, they literally ended each other's sentences.

The look in her eyes took him back to those days. But there was something else, as well. Fear? What in God's name could have been responsible for that?

"This is me, Lila. Brian. Talk to me. What's wrong?"

Lila lifted one shoulder in a half shrug, then let it drop. She valued his opinion of her. "I don't want you to think I'm an idiot."

"You're a lot of things, Lila, but you're not now, nor have you ever been, an idiot."

There was gratitude in her eyes when she smiled this time.

"Don't be that hasty to absolve me, Brian." She took a breath, then shook her head. She shouldn't have come. She was being a coward. There was no point in burdening him with this nonsense—and it was nonsense. Just crank calls, nothing more.

"No, never mind. You're busy and I'm letting my imagination run away with me." But as she started to get up, Brian caught her wrist, preventing her from making a quick getaway.

For a single moment the gentle pressure of his fingers against her skin generated a warmth that shot out in both directions from the point of contact. Her thoughts scattered even as she became acutely aware of how long it had been since there had been a strong man in her life. She was proud of her sons, fine officers both, but it wasn't the same thing as having a man to respect, to turn to, on a regular basis.

A man to be partners with in life.

Oh God, she thought, she was being overwrought. She needed to pull herself together. The sleepless nights were getting to her.

"You never had an imagination," he pointed out with a grin.

When he grinned like that, it took her back. Back to when they'd first met during a briefing session, her detective shield still warm from being issued. He was the veteran detective who balked at having such a "newbie" to work with. He was polite and respectful, but there was no actual on-the-job respect given her—until she'd earned it. Which she did, but it hadn't been easy.

And all the while, after putting in all those hours on the job, she would come home to Ben's unflattering implications that she was sharing more than just a working relationship with Brian. She put up with it as long as she could, assuring Ben that he was imagining things. Until the day she'd lashed out at him. Lashed out because, secretly, she had harbored thoughts about Brian, thoughts that could never go anywhere, could never see the light of day because they were both married and between them there were eight innocent kids to think of.

"We'll debate that some other time," she told him.

She was conscious of forcing a spasmodic smile to her lips. One look at Brian's face told her she wasn't fooling anyone. Okay, she was here, she might as well spit this out. He'd probably say something like it was nothing to worry about and she would be on her way.

Lila sat down again, perching on the edge of her seat. "I've been getting calls."

She captured his interest immediately. Lila wasn't the kind to spook. "What kind of calls?"

Lila watched his face for the first sign of annoyance or disappointment. Or was it already too late for that? "The hang-up kind."

His face appeared unreadable to her as he asked, "How often?"

She wasn't going to bore him with numbers, even though she had counted. It might make him think she was obsessing over nothing. "Often."

His eyes never left her face. "When did the calls start?"

She thought for a minute. "About five, six weeks ago. Always late at night," she added before he could ask. Why did things that happened in the night always seem so much more threatening? What was it about the lack of sunlight that made almost the simplest of things so unnerving?

"Some pervert?" Brian suggested.

"Possibly," Lila allowed, but he could tell by her tone that she didn't believe it. "There's no heavy breathing or anything. Just silence. But I know someone's there."

"Have you thought of changing your phone number?"

He saw her unconsciously square her shoulders. That was the Lila he knew, he thought, pleased to see her emerge. "That would be running."

"And you don't run." It wasn't a question. He knew that from experience.

"No, I don't." Lila frowned. "Look, it's my house. This—this person is invading it and I don't know why."

He asked the next logical question. "Have you told your kids about these phone calls?"

Her back was ramrod-straight, like a cadet coming to attention. "No. And you won't, either." Realizing that sounded as if she was ordering him around, Lila sighed and leaned back. She gave her own interpretation to his question. "You're right. I'm making too big a deal out of this. It probably is some pervert. Just because he doesn't breathe like someone who's just run across the finish line of the Los Angeles Marathon doesn't immediately exonerate him from being a weirdo." She was on her feet again. "Sorry I bothered you."

This time Brian stood up and moved in front of her, blocking her exit. "Is this a private conversation, or can anyone get in?"

Instead of laughing at the familiar assessment of her rapid-fire way of talking, for the first time since he'd known her, Lila McIntyre seemed flustered.

Chapter 2

"It's all that emptiness," Lila finally said after a long pause.

He'd been waiting for a response, but this didn't seem to connect with anything. Brian resisted the urge to put his arm around her waist and guide her back to the chair she'd just vacated. Lila always balked at being controlled, at least when they had been partnered together.

"Excuse me?" he asked.

Brian probably thought she sounded scattered, she thought. Hell, there were times when she *felt* scattered. Lila did her best to explain.

"The house is empty. Except for Duchess," she qualified. But although she loved the animal dearly, it just wasn't the same as having someone around to talk to, someone's presence to feel. She missed that, missed it something awful. People always talked about getting their lives back once their children moved out. But it just didn't seem like a fair trade-off to her. Having her kids around *was* her life. "The kids are on their own." She tried to make light of it. "Doesn't bother me so much during the day, but in the middle of the night…" Her voice trailed off as she shrugged.

She was trying to dismiss it. But he wasn't buying it. Lila wasn't the kind of woman to be afraid of things that went bump in the night. "You don't imagine the phone ringing."

Her eyes met his. "No," she replied quietly, "I don't."

"Then someone *is* calling you." Maybe she'd be more inclined to talk about it away from here, where everything felt so official. "Listen, do you want to get a cup of coffee?"

The question caught her by surprise. Eight years ago she would have merely nodded her head. Back then, grabbing a cup of coffee with Brian was as natural as breathing. But in the last eight years, by her own design, their paths had not crossed with any regularity. She felt a bit awkward just coming to him like this. It was as if she were trying to open up a part of her past that was supposed to have remained closed.

So instead of saying yes, she tried to demur. "You don't have to go out of your way."

Brian wasn't about to take no for an answer. As he'd told her a few minutes ago, there was nothing waiting for him at home and she made him curious. He'd always felt protective toward her, even though he knew there was a time when she would have skinned him alive if he would have voiced that out loud.

"I'm on my feet anyway, might as well walk toward the door." He did just that as he spoke. Placing his hand on the doorknob, he waited for her to follow. "The coffee shop isn't that far off."

Her mouth quirked as fragments of memories swirled through her head. "Neither is O'Malley's."

O'Malley's was where most of the detectives and uniforms at the station went to unwind and wash away some of the stench generated by the things they were forced to deal with. They did it so that they wouldn't bring the job home with them.

Brian inclined his head and grinned. It had been a while since he'd been to the watering hole. "Even better."

At that hour of the evening, O'Malley's was fairly unpopulated. One shift was gone and the next had not gotten off work yet. Only those from the previous shift, who had no one to go home to, could be found nursing a beer or trying to beat the odds at a game of pool. For them, O'Malley's was like a second home. At times, even better than the first.

Despite the lack of patrons and the dim lighting, Lila felt there was a cheerfulness about O'Malley's.

When she walked through the door, the bar seemed like an old friend who was happy to see her.

It had been a long while since she'd been here. The last time was when some of her friends had held an impromptu party, welcoming her back to the force. Against Ben's wishes, she'd gone back to work five years ago, when Frank graduated high school. But the focus of their lives, hers and her friends, was different now. She spent her day behind a desk, fighting a paper war while the people she'd known ever since her academy days were still on the streets in one capacity or another, either as uniformed patrol or detectives. They no longer had that much in common. But she'd kept her rank even though the work she did now didn't require the experience of a seasoned detective. At times she couldn't help wondering if pity had played any part in her retaining her rank.

"Still looks the same," Lila observed, more to herself than to the man beside her.

"That's why Shawn keeps the lights down low." As with the face of an old friend, Brian was so familiar with the place that, even after long absences, when he walked in, he really didn't see it. "Table or bar?" he asked, shutting the door behind them.

"Table."

"Table it is."

His hand to the small of her back, Brian steered his ex-partner toward a booth near the back of the room. He sensed she wanted privacy. Otherwise, she would have opted for a stool at the bar, the way she used to do when they frequented the place together.

"Beer?" he asked her as she slid into the booth.

Nodding, Lila slipped her purse from her shoulder. "Sounds good."

He caught himself watching as she took her seat. The woman still had the shapeliest legs he'd ever seen.

"Be right back," he promised.

She watched Brian as he walked over to the bar and placed their order with the man who methodically passed a cloth over one glass and then another. The glasses were lined up like crystal soldiers before him along the bar. He had a few more pounds on him than she remembered, but Lila recognized him immediately. Shawn O'Malley. His hair had some gray in it now, but he still looked powerful enough to take on any three rowdy customers with ease. An ex-cop, he retired early when a bullet sealed itself into his hip, defying excision. O'Malley's was his pride and joy, and he ruled the place like a benevolent king. He decided when someone had had enough. And everyone knew better than to argue with him.

Looking in her direction in response to something Brian said to him, Shawn raised one beefy hand in greeting, smiling his crooked smile at her. For just a second Lila felt as if no time at all had passed. In that second, the years melted away and she was a rookie again, a rookie eager to prove her worth and make the world a better, safer place because she was in it.

Where had the time gone? How could she possibly have gone from her twenties to her forties so damn fast? She didn't feel any older, she just was.

Shawn filled first one mug, then another, placing them on the bar. White foam topped off each serving, standing at attention even as he picked up one in each hand.

"Hi, stranger," Shawn called, rounding the bar and heading in her direction. His gait was just a bit lopsided in deference to the wound that had brought him to this place.

Brian walked beside the bartender. Reaching the booth, he slid in, taking the seat opposite her. Shawn placed the two mugs of beer on the table. He flashed her another wide smile as he presented her with her beer. "So where've you been keeping yourself all this time?"

She'd always liked talking to Shawn. He was like a cuddly bear. "I've been working at the precinct. Desk job," she added, watching his expression. She knew the man had no use for desk jobs. They'd offered him one after he'd been wounded and he had turned them down flat.

But Shawn merely nodded his shaggy head. "Can't hold that against you. Come by more often. We've missed that smile of yours." Straightening, he wiped his hands and winked as he nodded toward the mug in front of her. "It's on the house. Yours," he emphasized, then turned toward Brian. "Not yours. Your puss I get enough of."

Brian laughed. "If I'd have known that, I would have played more hard to get," he said before he took a sip of his beer.

"I'll leave you two to talk over old times. You get tired of Mr. Authority here—" Shawn jerked a thumb at Brian "—you know where to find me." The bartender began walking away and then he stopped. "Oh." He said the word as if a thought had suddenly found him. Or an afterthought. "I was sorry to hear about Ben."

It was on the tip of her tongue to ask what Shawn was sorry about hearing, that Ben was a suspect in the drug cartel debacle or that he had died much too soon. But that stirred up old wounds and she was in no frame of mind for that tonight. So she merely nodded.

"Thanks."

To curtail further conversation on that topic, Lila raised the mug to her lips and took a long sip of the bitter brew. The bartender crossed back to the bar and returned to polishing his glasses.

She was tense, Brian thought. He could see it in the corners of her mouth, in the slight furrow of the brow beneath her wispy bangs.

"You don't come by here anymore?" Brian asked mildly.

"I feel out of place. These are all real cops, out there fighting the good fight."

He knew there was more to it than that. There were people who thought that Ben had been turned, that he was a dirty cop who paid the ultimate penalty. By not coming here, Lila was avoiding those people. But they were in the minority, she had to know that. And even so, she wasn't to blame for what her husband had done. And neither were her kids.

Brian thought of pointing that out, then decided that he didn't want to open any wounds. Not until she indicated that she was ready for that.

"Those also serve who push paper around," he quipped. "Besides," he went on, growing serious, "you did more than your part. A little more to the right and you wouldn't be here right now."

A cold shiver slithered down her spine the way it always did whenever she thought of that incident. Brian referred to the bullet that had ended her active career. How like him to take himself out of the equation when it came to taking credit.

"If it wasn't for you, I wouldn't be here," she corrected. "You're the one who saved my life, Brian." Her eyes shifted to the hands that were wrapped around his beer mug. A fond smile played on her lips. "You and those big hands of yours."

Brian glanced down at them as if he'd just now noticed that they were a part of him. The incident vividly came back to him. He'd never been so scared before in his life. Without any effort at all, he could almost feel her warm blood pouring out of the hole, the hole he frantically pressed his fingers against. Waiting for the paramedics to arrive had been the longest ten minutes of his life.

"Susan used to say they were too big, too clumsy."

"Susan never appreciated what she had." Before the words were out, Lila regretted them. It wasn't her place to criticize the man's wife, especially now that she was gone. "Sorry, I shouldn't have said that."

"Because she killed herself?" There, he thought, he laid it out in the open. Now they could get past it. "We all have our demons."

"Amen to that," she said softly.

She kept glancing around, he noticed. As if she expected someone to turn up. Someone she knew. Was she worried that one of her sons or daughters would walk in and see her? What difference would it make?

Very carefully, Brian took the mug of beer from her and placed it off to the side on the table, then took her hands in his. Her expression never changed, but he could feel her tensing.

"There's nobody here who knows you. Except Shawn, and he always had a soft spot for you. Not Ben," he allowed truthfully, "but you."

He didn't add that the reason for that didn't have anything to do with the rumors about Ben selling out. It was because both he and Shawn, as well as a few others, were privy to the fact that Ben had stepped out on Lila more than once. Handsome to a fault, Ben McIntyre took advantage of the fact that he attracted women like a rock star attracted adoring fans.

Realizing that he was still holding her hands, Brian released them. Questions kept cropping up in his head, so many questions. He didn't even know where to start. But he knew he needed to put her at ease if he hoped to get any answers. For the moment, he pushed aside the reason she'd sought him out. There was time enough for that later. Brian already knew what he was going to do about her problem.

Leaning over the table, his eyes on hers, he asked in the friendliest voice he could generate, "So how have you been?"

Lonely. "Busy," she told him out loud. "I actually do like the work, although not as much as being out in the field," she qualified honestly. "Wayne Langtree's wife just had a baby and he took off some time to be with his new family, so we're pretty swamped."

Brian smiled to himself as he shook his head in wonder. "Maternity leave for men. Who would have thought it? There's a whole new world out there now, Lila. It was a hell of a lot different when we first came on the job." For one thing, he thought, there hadn't been all that many women in uniform, much less carrying a detective's shield. Lila had a lot to be proud of. "The world is really changing, Lila." He thought of all the bureaucracy that had come into existence, bureaucracy that at times got in the way of honest cops doing their jobs. He shook his head. "Sometimes I don't know if that's good or bad."

That made two of them, Lila thought. "Some things don't change," she reminded him. She saw him raise an eyebrow, waiting for her to elaborate. "There are still bad guys out there for you to catch."

"Not me," he said, and she was certain she heard more than a slight note of regret.

The same sort of regret she felt, watching her children suit up for work while she went in to spend her days behind a desk. What she did was necessary, but there was nothing like the rush that came from knowing you'd saved someone's life or that you'd stopped a murderer from killing again.

"That's for the others to do." His eyes met hers. He could see his former partner in there. The one he'd shared so many thoughts with. "You know, sometimes I really miss the old days."

Something almost electrical zipped through her.

Lila cleared her throat, looking away. Who would have thought, after all this time, that she would still feel this pull, this magnetism dancing between them? This "thing" that went beyond the friendship she and he had forged over the six-year course of their working relationship?

After everything that she had been through, it was still there, still alive.

Maybe for you, but what about him?

She wasn't prepared to find out.

"Me, too," she agreed. Did he suspect? Did part of him know how she'd once felt about him? How she probably still felt about him? Banking down her thoughts, she took refuge in her children. It was a safe move. "I miss having the kids all living at home—I even miss the arguments."

"Not sure I'd go that far." Brian laughed. "But I do miss the sound of someone breathing in the house besides me."

About to take another sip of her beer, she stopped and nodded vigorously. "Oh God, yes. Of course the dog's there, but it's not the same thing. I love her dearly, but she just doesn't hold her own in a conversation." Brian laughed. She'd forgotten how much she liked the sound of his laughter. It was warm and rich and deep. And disarming. She heard herself saying, "You know what's the worst? When I wake up from a nightmare and still think they're living at home. When the realization sinks in that they're not, it's just awful."

"I know exactly what you mean." He paused for a moment, debating whether or not to ask and if she'd considered it prying. He assuaged his conscience by telling himself that friends didn't pry, they expressed concern. "You have nightmares?"

Maybe she shouldn't have said that. He was going to think she'd become a drama queen. Like his wife. Too late now, she thought. He was obviously waiting for her to elaborate.

"Sometimes," she finally admitted.

"About anything in particular?"

Yes, about Ben. About the way he looked when he washed up on shore. But out loud, she said, "About that night." It wasn't a lie. Sometimes she had nightmares about that. But not nearly as often as the other. "It never quite leaves me."

Life had changed quickly after that night. They had never really had a chance to talk about it. Ben was always standing guard, limiting his access to Lila. And then she'd left the force and he'd gone on to become the chief of detectives. And a widower.

"Maybe you should have gone to the department shrink," he suggested tactfully, knowing it wasn't what she wanted to hear, but maybe it was something she needed to hear. He saw her closing up before his eyes.

"Ben didn't have any use for shrinks."

Husband or not, Brian never got the sense that the man had her best interests at heart. "Ben wasn't the one who got shot."

"No, not then," she said softly.

Damn, he'd walked right into that one with his size-twelve feet. How could he have not remembered? There'd been a bullet to the head at close range. "I'm sorry. That just came out. I didn't mean—"

She didn't want him feeling guilty. Not when he'd always been there for her. "I know you didn't."

She was right not to tell him about the other nightmares. The ones about Ben being shot, about his being beaten and tortured and clubbed in the face. His teeth were all destroyed in an obvious ploy to hide his identity on the off chance that his body would wash up on shore. Which it had.

Lila could shut it down during the day, but at night, it was a different story. Asleep, she envisioned all of it on a recurring basis.

That, too, made her hate going to sleep in the empty house.

Brian could almost see her pulling away. He knew her well enough, even now, to pick up on the signs. Maybe it was time to revert back to why she'd sought him out. "About this not-so-heavy breather of yours—"

Lila waved her hand, dismissing the topic. "Forget it."

"No," he replied in the soft, no-nonsense voice that his detectives had learned could not be opposed. "I won't. It was important enough for you to break your self-imposed exile and come look me up."

Because it was more than a little true, she took exception to his words. "There was no self-imposed exile."

"Then why have you been avoiding me all this time?"

Shrugging, she went for the obvious. "We work on different floors."

"But not different countries," he pointed out. "Last time I looked, the station had elevators and a phone system. I know, I used both." When he heard she was back and then again when Ben had been murdered, he'd tried to get in touch with her. To no avail. "And every time I tried to get in contact with you, you were either dashing off somewhere or your machine would pick up. Eventually, even someone as thick-headed as me takes the hint."

"There were no hints," she insisted, feeling guilty

about having treated him that way. Feeling guiltier about lying now. "I was just busy."

"Twenty-four, seven?"

She was in too deep to abandon the lie now. "Twenty-five, eight," Lila countered. What good would it do either of them for him to know that she hadn't been up to facing him, not up to having to defend her husband to someone who'd once been her best friend?

Would all that ever be completely behind her? Would she ever be able to be as open with Brian as she once had been? God, she hoped so.

"I'm not as fast as I used to be," she told him.

One eyebrow rose in a silent, skeptical declaration. "Ha. That'll be the day. There is no slowing you down."

He made her laugh. He always made her laugh, she recalled. Even when things at home were unbearable, she could always count on Brian to divert her for a little while, to come through and make things seem better.

She looked at him now and wondered if she could still count on him. Or if, ultimately, time had changed that, too.

Chapter 3

The next words out of his mouth told her that her faith had not been misplaced.

"I'm going to have a tap put on your phone," Brian told her. "See if we can find out who this night caller of yours is and 'politely' suggest he get his entertainment some other way—or face prosecution."

She didn't want it to come to that. She just wanted it to stop. More than likely, it was someone who thought she was somehow involved in the mess that had ended Ben's life. So many rumors abounded around that time. Some had her killing Ben herself and using the drug cartel scandal as cover. Others thought she was as deeply involved as they said Ben was, taking money from the drug dealers to look the other way. There were as many different rumors as days of the week. She learned not to pay attention to any of them and waited for the air to clear. And eventually it did. But some rumors died harder than others.

She wondered if Brian had been tempted to believe any of them. But this wasn't the time to ask. So she nodded in response to his offer.

"I'd appreciate it." And then she hesitated. "Brian, you won't..."

"Tell anyone?" he guessed. "I'll have to tell the guy running the tap, but I'll swear him to secrecy," he quipped. "I'd offer to blindfold him if you like, but then he might not do the best job."

Brian smiled at her understandingly. He could only guess at what she'd gone through. If she hadn't been so damn stubborn, he might have been able to help long before this. But then, he supposed, she wouldn't have been Lila. Independent as hell.

"It'll be off the record," he assured her. He saw a hint of skepticism in her eyes. "You don't put in as much time on the force as I have without gathering a few favors to call in."

He liked the way relief softened her expression. "I really appreciate this, Brian," she repeated. "I know you probably think I'm overreacting."

"Lila, when we were partners, I learned to respect your gut instincts. You never overreacted then and you're probably not overreacting now."

She caught the one word he had glossed over. "'Probably.'"

Brian smiled. The wording was a result of on-the-job indoctrination. "Being the chief of d's has taught me to be cautious."

Brian set down his mug, finished with his beer, but she was still nursing hers. "Well, I'm glad something finally did. For a man with four kids, you were always a little reckless," she remembered, then took another long swig of the amber brew.

As he recalled their partnership, Lila was always the one to rush in where angels feared to go, not him. "Look who's talking."

She had the good grace not to argue. "Maybe you have a point."

Folding his hands before him, he watched her for a long moment. Humor faded in the face of more serious memories. "If you'd been a little less gung ho, I would have been the one who caught the bullet that night. And a lot of things might have been different." For one thing, she would have continued on the job and he would have refused to retire, the way Ben had made her do. They would have continued working together and she would have never withdrawn from him.

Lila could almost hear what he was thinking. No point in going there, that path led nowhere. So she did her best to lighten the moment. "Yeah, you would have been dead because blood makes me squeamish. I could have never done what you did, put my hand over the hole to try to get it to stop bleeding."

Brian knew better. Knew that when they were partnered, she had always been there for him. That she had his back no matter what.

"Somehow, I don't think so." He paused for a moment, debating whether to take on more serious subjects. There was so much to talk about. So much to try to catch up on. Even after their partnership had terminated, even after she clearly began to avoid him—because of Ben, he'd like to believe—he'd thought about her. Thought about her a lot if he were being honest with himself. He'd wondered what she was doing, how she was getting along and if he should take it upon himself to barrage into her self-imposed solitude.

He never did. Maybe he should have. Because God knew he'd missed her.

Impulse, something he rarely experienced and even more rarely gave in to, had him asking, "Listen, would you like to have dinner sometime?"

Lila's mouth curved slowly, like a flower responding to the first rays of the summer sun. "Sometime," she echoed.

Heartened, Brian pressed on. "How about tomorrow night?"

She blinked. "'Sometime' came fast."

He spread his hands, taking care not to knock over the empty mug. "Hey, if this business has taught me nothing else, it's that you never know how much time you have left—" he eyed her intently "—and personally, I think that I've lost too much time with my best friend already."

Best friend. He probably had no idea how comforting that sounded to her. Or how much she had missed him, Lila thought.

"Me, too," she agreed softly. And then, because she thought that maybe she'd admitted too much, she focused on what he'd said about the capricious nature of the kind of life police officers led. "When the kids all opted to go into the force, I was both so proud and so scared. A big part of me just wanted them to be safe. To sit in cubicles where nothing more serious than a paper cut threatened them."

"You sit in a cubicle," he reminded her, humor framing his mouth. "How do you like it?"

Lila laughed. Checkmate—or was it touché? she wondered. In any case, he had her. "I hate it."

He nodded, knowing that she did. He couldn't help wondering why, after Ben had died and the man's hold over her went with him, she hadn't asked to be put back in the field in some capacity.

"Wouldn't wish an existence they'd hate on your kids, would you?"

"No." Which was why she'd never told even her daughters, Riley and Taylor, how she felt about their choice of a vocation. "But I still get knots in my stomach at times, worrying."

"All parents worry—if they're worth their salt." It was a given. He worried about all of his kids, even

Janelle, who was an assistant to the D.A. All of them dealt with the criminal element every day. There was nothing reassuring about that. But some things were just out of his hands.

However, the direction of the conversation was not and he got it back on track. "So, what's your answer?"

Lila raised her eyes to his quizzically. Something quivered in his gut. "My answer?"

She did innocent well, Brian thought, amused. "I wasn't distracted by the sidebar, Lila. Dinner? Tomorrow?"

Lila moved the mug aside. She'd had enough beer. Taking in a breath, she let it out slowly, as if by doing so it somehow signaled the beginning of a new journey. One that promised to be far more pleasant than the one she'd just been on.

"Dinner. Tomorrow," she echoed, confirming the engagement.

Something like the burst of sunshine went off in his chest. He didn't try to explore the reasons behind it. "Great. I'll pick you up at your place. Seven o'clock all right?"

Now that she was living alone, dinner no longer had a set time. It was dictated by the contents of her refrigerator and her desire to nibble.

"Seven o'clock is fine," she assured him. Warmth spread through her as she felt him looking at her. She wasn't quite sure how to handle this, so she pushed it aside for the time being. Glancing at her watch, she realized that a lot more time had gone by than she'd thought. "I'd better get going." She flashed him a grateful smile. "I've kept you long enough."

He began to protest that it hadn't been nearly long enough, then thought better of it. She was still skittish, even though that was difficult to reconcile with the Lila he knew. So instead, he rose from the booth, signaling that he was ready to go, too.

As Lila slid out, he leaned over to quietly tell her, "The tap will be put in place tomorrow morning. I'll send Manny Lopez over." The senior computer tech was both exceptionally competent and quiet. "What time do you leave for work?"

The precinct was only ten minutes away, but she liked getting in early. "Seven-thirty."

"Manny will be there at seven." It was before his shift, but he knew he could prevail on the man to come in early. "It shouldn't take long."

"Are you sure he won't mind putting in the extra time?"

Manny, a widower, had a daughter who had been caught shoplifting last year. Brian had made the charges go away, keeping them off the police blotter in exchange for Rachel "volunteering" for community service and counseling.

Nodding, she preceded Brian as they made their way to the door.

"Come back soon," Shawn called after them.

Brian glanced over his shoulder toward the bartender. "Count on it."

"I'm talking to the cute blonde, not you, Cavanaugh," Shawn responded.

Lila laughed and raised her hand above her head to wave goodbye.

"You have an admirer," Brian told her as they walked out.

"Shawn was always a good guy." She turned around at the entrance. The night air was chilly. The temperature had dropped drastically since they'd gone inside. Lila turned up her collar, wrapping her arms around herself. "So are you, Brian."

Then why had she avoided him? But he knew better than to ask the question this early in their reconnection. If he did, she might find a reason to cancel tomorrow night. And he was really looking forward to tomorrow night.

"Hang on to that thought," he told her as they walked back to the precinct parking lot.

He was whistling when he got home twenty minutes later. Even walking into the dark house didn't bother him the way it usually did.

Ordinarily, the darkness and silence assaulted him the second he pushed open the front door. But not tonight. Tonight, this was the house where a lot of living had gone on, where four babies had grown up to be upstanding adults.

And where, tonight, he felt like a kid again.

Though Brian had never looked toward each birthday with increasing dread, he could feel his usual zest for life waning these last few months.

Maybe it was because everyone in his family had now paired off. That didn't just include his own kids but Andrew's and Mike's, as well. Eleven members in all, every one of them married and in the family way—or getting there. Even Andrew, who had been on his own for so many years, was now reunited with the wife only he had actually believed was still alive.

Rose Cavanaugh had disappeared one morning after an argument with her husband. All the evidence had pointed to her death, not the least of which was the fact that her car was discovered in the river. Her body wasn't found, but it could have easily been swept out to sea, and that was what everyone believed.

Everyone but Andrew.

He never gave up hope, and over the years, every spare moment he had found him poring over one dead end after another, until he *finally* found her. But even that hadn't been a total success. Rose had been working at a diner upstate and was a victim of amnesia. She had no recollection of the husband and children she'd left behind.

Undaunted, Andrew displayed ultimate patience and somehow got her to come around, to remember.

So there they all were, paired up and happy while he pretended it didn't matter to him that he was always stag at the endless family functions.

Well, tomorrow night he wasn't going to go stag. Tomorrow he was going out with Lila.

"Don't go getting ahead of yourself," he murmured to himself. Methodically, he removed his jacket and then his holster with the service revolver. The former he slung across the back of a chair, but he placed the latter on the third shelf of his bookcase, the way he had been doing for the past twenty-some-odd years. "It's just dinner, just catching up on old times."

And maybe, finally, making a few new ones, he added silently.

"You talking to yourself now?"

Reaching for his gun, Brian swung around toward the sound of the voice, the weapon aimed and ready to fire. Andrew was standing in the doorway, looking more amused than angry or distressed.

"Easy, Quick Draw." Andrew raised one hand in mock surrender.

Putting the safety back on, Brian returned the gun to its holster. "How did you get in here?"

"The front door was open." Andrew nodded in the general direction of the door. "You forgot to lock it." He crossed over toward Brian. "Not like you to be absentminded." He considered his assessment for a second. "'Course, not like you to be talking to yourself, either. Hope you don't do that down at the precinct. Wouldn't want people to start talking, saying that my little brother is going crazy. Might not reflect well on the rest of the family. Or the police force for that matter, having a chief of d's who talks to himself."

He couldn't care less what people at the station

gossiped about. People always found something to talk about. All he cared about was what his family thought of him—and what he thought of himself. "Why don't you let me worry about what people say about me?"

To his surprise, Andrew shook his head. "Can't. I'm the patriarch of the family, remember? That's what patriarchs do, they worry about the family's reputation."

Brian didn't have any experience with so-called patriarchs, but he knew Andrew and what was important to his older brother. It wasn't necessarily reputation, but seeing to it that everyone was fed. Well fed. "And cook."

"If they're exceptional," Andrew deadpanned. "And speaking of food," he continued, "that leads me to what I'm doing here."

Brian crossed his arms before him, his affection for his brother more than slightly apparent. "I figured you'd get around to it, sooner or later."

"I've come to take you to dinner."

He'd wondered when Andrew would finally swoop down on him. It was very important to his older brother to have family members turn up at his table on at least a semi-regular basis and he'd been absent of late.

Still, he couldn't resist giving Andrew a hard time. "I don't remember you asking."

Andrew looked at him as if he'd taken leave of his senses. "It's a standing invitation. That means I don't have to ask."

Brian parried to Andrew's thrust. "That also means

if I don't show up, no one's nose is supposed to be bent out of joint."

"Yours might be if you give me a hard time," Andrew informed him. "Rose told me not to come home without you."

Brian knew better. Although he and his sister-in-law got along very well, it was Andrew who insisted on meal attendance, Andrew who found any kind of an excuse to throw an immense family party, Andrew who insisted that the family that ate together, stayed together.

"Or what," Brian asked, amused, "she'll give you a time-out?"

Andrew ignored the question, getting down instead to the reason he'd come to fetch his brother. "You haven't been around for a couple of weeks."

He knew families who only saw one another over the holidays, if then. But to Andrew, that was unthinkable, and now that he reflected on it, Brian had to admit that he was grateful that he was a part of this family rather than the other kind.

But he did enjoy giving Andrew a hard time. "Maybe I'm on a diet."

Andrew never missed a beat. "I've got carrots sticks. You can gnaw on a few while the rest of us eat." Looking around the house, Andrew frowned. "You spend too much time alone."

Amen to that. But he wasn't about to make noises like a grieving woman after the last of her children had moved out. It just wasn't manly. "Ever think I might want to be alone?"

Andrew shook his head. "No. You're too much like me. Let's face it, we're family men, not lone wolves."

The description struck a chord. "Like Mike?" Brian asked.

Their middle brother, killed on the job years ago, had been the different one, the one who had been out of step with the rest of them. A policeman, as well, he spent his life living in the shadow of both his older brother and his younger one, never finding a place for himself other than in a bottle. And never learning to appreciate the two young souls he'd help bring into the world. Andrew'd had more to do with raising Patience and Patrick even when Mike was alive than Mike did.

"Mike couldn't help being what he was."

There, they had a difference of opinion. Andrew was being too lax. "Everyone can help being what they are. You can't help being tall, or right-handed, but you can do something about what you feel inside."

"Fascinating," Andrew declared with feeling as he slipped his arm around his brother's shoulder. "Why don't you elaborate on that, say, over dinner? Really," he added seriously, "I hate thinking of you rattling around in this place night after night, standing over the sink or sitting in front of the TV, eating out of a can—"

"Take-out," Brian corrected. "I eat take-out food."

Andrew shuddered. "Even worse." He played his

ace card. "I've got a pot roast waiting. It's got your name on it."

Brian laughed. "You know, the sad thing is, I don't doubt that. I can just see you carving my name into it."

"Why would I bother to lie, especially since I outrank you?"

"You can't outrank me. You're the 'former' police chief, remember? You retired."

Andrew hit the back of Brian's head with the flat of his hand, as if to knock some sense into him. "I'm talking about in the family hierarchy."

Brian rubbed the back of his head more for show than out of any sense of injury. "You always did have a way with words."

"And pot roast."

"And pot roast," Andrew agreed, following his brother out the door.

Chapter 4

Dinner turned out to be just the two of them. Rose was out with her daughters and daughters-in-law for a rare ladies' night out. Brian had a feeling that his brother would have probably preferred a ladies' night in instead. After all that he had been through, raising his family on his own and always searching for news of Rose, Andrew deserved to reap the rewards of his efforts.

But this gave them a chance to just kick back and talk. After the pot roast had been served and devoured, Andrew felt their "talk" hadn't become substantive enough.

Picking up the last of the dishes, Andrew deposited

them into the dishwasher. He took his drink of choice—whiskey—and two shot glasses from the cupboard and placed them on the coffee table between them. He poured two fingers' worth into each glass and nudged Brian's over to him. Brian nodded as he raised the glass to his lips.

Andrew waited until the first sharp jolt had worked its way down his brother's throat and spread its unique band of fire. "Okay, what's up?"

Brian narrowed his eyes. "What's up with what?"

"My question exactly," Andrew said.

Amusement caused Brian to arch one eyebrow as he continued studying his brother. He took another sip of the whiskey. Damn, but it had kick to it. "You've been sniffing your spices again, Drew. You're not making any sense."

Andrew tossed back his own drink, then set the glass down beside the cut-glass decanter, a gift from his two oldest on his forty-fifth birthday. "All right, I'll spell it out for you. I know my pot roast is out of this world, but it never made you grin from ear to ear like a goofy schoolboy before."

Brian laughed shortly. "And you wonder why I don't come over more often."

"Stop stalling. I raised five kids, I ran a large precinct, I know when something's up. Spill it."

Because there were times that he liked controlling the situation, even when his brother was involved, Brian studied his shot glass for a moment. He decided to take the long way around the answer just to drive Andrew crazy. There wasn't anything he wouldn't do for his older brother, but that didn't mean he liked having him nosing around in his business.

"I won't be available for dinner tomorrow night."

That was already a given. "Not that I figured you'd come here twice in two days without being forcibly escorted, but you're not going to be available because…?" Andrew's voice trailed off as he waited for his brother to finish the sentence.

Brian finished the last of his drink instead. When Andrew raised the decanter to refill his glass again, he shook his head. One was his limit unless he was staying over. "I'll be eating dinner elsewhere."

Andrew set the decanter down again after giving himself just one finger's worth. "Where, damn it?"

Brian deliberately assumed an innocent expression. "At a restaurant."

Andrew's steely blue-gray eyes bore into his. "Not alone?"

Brian's expression never changed. "Not alone."

Andrew blew out a breath. When necessary, he could be the most patient of people, extracting information at the rate of a single syllable a minute. But this was not one of those times.

He scowled at his younger brother. "I still have my service revolver somewhere," he reminded Brian. When he'd gone in for early retirement to take care of his then motherless children, the powers that be at the police department had allowed him to keep his weapon out of respect for his selfless service to the force and the people of Aurora. "Don't make me shoot you. Who are you not being alone with?"

Brian did his best not to laugh at the twisted sentence. "Lila McIntyre." Now that the information was out, he expected Andrew to say something like, "Finally" or "Thank God." His older brother had been after him to start seeing women the moment Rose came back into his own life. With all the Cavanaugh offspring married off, getting him together with someone had become almost a crusade for the self-appointed patriarch.

So when Brian saw a thoughtful frown forming on Andrew's face, he was more than a little surprised.

"What's the matter, am I ruining some kind of dinner plans you had for the family?" When Andrew threw a party, family attendance was mandatory. Andrew accepted few excuses, insisting that whatever other plans were in the offing could keep. Back when their children were still in the dating stages of their lives, Andrew would invite whoever they were seeing at the time to the party, as well.

No one was able to say no to Andrew and make it stick.

Andrew set aside his drink. He leaned forward, his expression devoid of any humor. This was serious. "You know that there were rumors going around at the time that she killed Ben and actually staged that thing with the drug cartel to make it look as if it was a revenge killing."

While it was happening, they'd never discussed either Ben or Lila, never even broached the subject. Brian always assumed it was because Andrew was being thoughtful of his feelings, knowing that he and Lila had a bond.

Brian's voice gave away nothing. "I'm aware of the rumors."

Andrew nodded, his eyes searching his brother's face for things left unsaid. "Just so you know."

He couldn't live with himself if he just let it drop here. Did Andrew actually believe that Lila was capable of murder? Was he *serious?*

"I also know that they can't possibly be true." He thought of Ben, of the animosity the man generated. Lila remained loyal, never complaining about her husband, but he'd picked up on things and knew there were problems. "Not that the bastard didn't deserve it."

"No argument," Andrew agreed, "but don't let any-one else hear you say that."

Brian suddenly felt the need for another drink, a stiff one, but then he'd have to wait to go home and he needed to be leaving soon. "Ben McIntyre was a bully and everyone knew it. If he hadn't been killed, Internal Affairs was set to have him investigated." He took a breath. He didn't want to waste time talking about a man he'd never liked. But he didn't want Andrew thinking badly of his old partner. She deserved better. "Lila was my partner and I trusted her with my life every day we clocked in together. I wouldn't have done that if she wasn't stable."

Andrew's eyes held his. "Even stable people kill when pushed too far." They both knew that. Everyone had a breaking point. And, off the record, God knew she'd put up with a lot from Ben.

Brian tried to lighten the mood. "So what are you saying, I should bring my service revolver to dinner with me in case she has a fit?"

Andrew spread his hands wide. "I just don't want you putting blinders on."

Okay now Andrew was talking in riddles, Brian thought. "Blinders?"

"Yes, blinders," he repeated. "Because you care about her."

Brian balked. "Of course I care about her. She was my partner for six years."

Andrew looked at him knowingly. They both knew what he was talking about, even if Brian didn't want to admit it. "There's more to it than that and you know it."

Just what was it that Andrew was implying? Back then, Lila was married and so was he. Neither one of them ever cheated on their vows. "Nothing ever happened between us."

"I didn't say it did. But it could have," Andrew added quietly. "And nobody would have blamed either one of you."

Brian looked away. "I liked you better when you were pushing pot roast."

"Sorry." The word rang flat, devoid of any feeling, because Andrew wasn't sorry that he cared. It was just the way things were. "I worry about you. Comes with the territory."

"Yeah, yeah." Brian knew his brother meant well. He supposed he was just being edgy—and protective of Lila. "Next time around, I'm volunteering to be the oldest."

Andrew laughed shortly. "Good luck with that." Brian rose and he rose with him. "And don't get me wrong, I like Lila. I just want you to be aware of all the facts."

"All the rumors," Brian corrected as he began to walk toward the front door. "Not facts, rumors. Nothing was ever proven," he reminded Andrew. "Not even that Ben was a dirty cop. He was undercover when he died, remember? Much as I didn't like the guy, we both know that being undercover sometimes means doing things you wouldn't normally do or want to do to avoid blowing your cover."

Andrew paused before the door. "They never found the money that was meant for the buy, either."

"No, they didn't. Since both Ben and his partner were found executed, my guess is that someone else took it. Someone who engineered the whole 'dirty cop' tempest to throw everyone else off the trail. Nobody found any proof that Ben was on the take," he said, being fair even though he would have rather left the man's character painted in black strokes. "No offshore bank accounts in his name, no extravagant purchases, nothing to make him look guilty."

"Walker was," Andrew recalled. A minor drug dealer had stepped forward soon after Ben's partner's body had been found, pointing a finger at the dead detective.

Brian hated the fact that he was actually defending Lila's late husband. But in all honesty, he couldn't do anything else until evidence to the contrary came to light.

"Dean Walker was Ben's partner, but that doesn't mean that Ben was dirty by association." The subject left a bad taste in his mouth. Time to close it. "We've been through that kind of garbage ourselves. I'm almost fifty years old, Drew. I don't need a big brother looking after me. I need a friend."

"Sorry, but it's a package deal." And this time, Andrew smiled. "I'll see what I can do about restraining the brother thing. Say, I've got an idea, why don't you bring Lila here? I've just found this really exotic recipe for—"

"No. If it's all the same to you, I'd rather not have my date interrogated."

Andrew's eyes crinkled. "So, it's a date, not just dinner and catching up."

Brian swung open the door and stepped over the threshold. "Good night, Andrew. Thanks for the pot roast."

Andrew laughed. It was good spending time with just Brian. He was glad he'd gone out of his way to bring him over. "Good night, Brian."

Brian was already making his way down the driveway. "And give my sympathy to Rose when she gets home," he tossed over his shoulder. "How she puts up with you is more than I can understand."

"It's because I'm so charming," Andrew called after him.

Brian waved his hand over his head, dismissing Andrew's claim without bothering to turn around. "Yeah, right."

The mascara brush slipped from her fingers. For the second time.

Lila sighed as she bent to pick it up again. This was silly. Why in heaven's name was she so nervous? She was just going to have a simple dinner with an old friend, that's all. A night out for a change instead of sitting at home in front of the television set, stroking Duchess's head as she watched a forgettable program.

If this was just a simple dinner, why were there five different outfits spread out on her bed, haphazardly discarded one by one as she found something wrong with each one?

Stepping back from the bureau, she retired the mascara brush and surveyed herself.

All wrong.

With determination, she returned to her closet and dug into the recesses one more time. She pulled out an aqua-colored dress and held it against herself. It had possibilities, she decided as she quickly stripped off the two-piece outfit she was currently wearing. The skirt pooled at her feet and she kicked it aside. The pullover was next.

More than likely, Brian wouldn't even notice what she was wearing. Men didn't notice that about women her age. Their attention only perked up when they were in the vicinity of some nubile twenty-year-olds.

Brian wasn't like that, she silently insisted, looking herself over with a critical eye. Brian noticed things, noticed details. It was what had made him such a damn good detective.

She frowned. Maybe she should go back to the first outfit. Oh God. Her head jerked around toward the sound she heard. Was that him?

Someone was ringing her doorbell.

He was early.

Quickly, Lila scooped up all the clothes from her bed and jammed them into the closet. She'd worry about hanging them up later.

Earrings, she needed earrings. Or earring, she amended, realizing that she'd put one on and then gotten distracted from putting on the second one.

She plucked it from the bureau and quickly slipped on her shoes. The back of her left shoe didn't quite make it on, but she was already hurrying down the stairs.

Duchess, who'd been privy to her frantic search through her wardrobe, now clattered down the carpeted stairs right behind her, determined to discover what had sent her mistress into such an uncustomary tizzy.

"I thought you said seven," Lila protested as she pulled open the front door, her heart insisting on going into double-time.

Instead of Brian on her doorstep, there was just empty space.

"Brian?" But even as she said his name, she could feel a tightness beginning in her throat. A premonition, like the old days. Like the one she'd had just before she'd taken that bullet that had probably been meant for Brian.

Taking a step out onto the welcome mat, Lila looked both left and then right. And saw no one.

The uneasiness that found her each time she received one of those silent phone calls descended on her. In spades.

Was it the same person? Had he escalated what he was doing?

Why was someone doing this? Was he—or she— trying to drive her out of the house?

Or out of her mind?

Maybe she should consider selling the house. Rita Nunez, someone she knew from the precinct back in the old days, had approached her with an offer just a couple of weeks ago. Maybe she'd been too hasty, turning her down. After all, she'd always said that once the children were gone, having this much space would depress her.

No, this was her home and she was staying. This way, there was always enough room if the kids decided they wanted to stay over, like at Christmas.

Lila tried to calm herself down. Her heart continued racing. This was more than a prank, she could feel it in her bones.

Back across the threshold again, she closed the door firmly and then, after a beat, looked down at the animal who had remained silently inside the house when she'd looked around outside.

"Falling down on the job, Duchess? You're supposed to bark when strangers come to the door, not sit there like a big stuffed animal."

As if in response, Duchess suddenly began barking in earnest, her attention focused on the front door.

"Now you're barking." Lila threw up her hands. But the dog continued, making her pause. "Is there someone at the door, girl?"

The next second, the doorbell rang and Lila nearly jumped out of her skin. Duchess barked louder. Lila hurried over to the bookcase where she kept her service revolver. Taking it out of the holster and flipping off the safety, she crossed back to the front door just in time to hear the doorbell again.

Braced, she swung the door open with one hand, her gun, ready to use, in the other.

This time, she wasn't looking into the empty air or the face of a malevolent stranger.

Brian stood on her doorstep, warily eyeing the weapon pointed at his chest.

"Change your mind about dinner?" he quipped.

Lila exhaled a loud sigh of relief, the rigid tension

melting from her body. She retired the hammer on her gun and put the safety back on.

Motioning him in, she turned away and crossed back to the bookcase. "I thought you were someone else."

Obviously not someone she wanted to see, he thought. "Who?"

Returning the gun to its holster, she tucked it away and turned around to look at Brian. "That's just it, I don't know. My anonymous caller," she guessed. She knew she sounded as if she was babbling and backtracked. "Just before you came, there was someone at the door. They rang the bell."

Brian hadn't seen anyone just now when he pulled up, but then, he hadn't been looking for anyone, either. "And?"

Lila shrugged helplessly. "They were gone by the time I opened it. Just like with the telephone." She looked up at him to see if he thought she was crazy.

What she saw on his face was not skepticism but concern. "You know, I can have someone stay with you." In fact, he'd prefer it.

But Lila shook her head, vetoing the idea. "Brian, I'm a policewoman. Just because I sit behind a desk doesn't mean that I don't remember how to take care of myself."

She was touchy, he knew that. "I'm not saying that, but *I'd* feel a hell of a lot better if someone was here with you."

Like a wet nurse, she thought, frustrated. Maybe she

shouldn't have come to him for help in the first place.
"I wouldn't."

Duchess was circling him now, sniffing his pant legs
from all angles as if to determine whether or not he was
trustworthy. "Safety in numbers," Brian insisted.
"Maybe one of your sons—"

"No," she said firmly. "I said I didn't want them
brought into this."

"Then one of my sons," he countered. "Or one of
Andrew's daughters—" He didn't care who it was as
long as there was someone else here with her, someone
with two feet rather than four, he thought, glancing at
the circling, aging German shepherd.

"I don't need a babysitter," Lila told him flatly. She
looked tense again. "I thought you were here to take me
out, not lecture me."

He knew what worked with her and what didn't. For
a moment, his concern had made him forget that when
it came to her own safety, Lila had to be dealt with with
kid gloves. She couldn't be bullied into anything.

With a nod, he opened the door and went out again.

Was he leaving? "Where are you going?" Lila
cried, surprised.

Brian turned back around to face her before he
answered. "I'm starting over. You want to close the
door so I can ring the doorbell again?"

Her tension dissipated as swiftly as it had come.
Laughing, she grabbed hold of his arm and pulled him
back inside.

"Not necessary. Wait here," she told him. "I'll get my purse."

Brian leaned against the doorsill. Duchess had stopped circling and sniffing. She now stood on the scatter rug just inside the foyer, looking up at him and panting. He scratched her behind the ear. The way her foot thumped, he knew he had a friend for life.

"Will you be bringing the gun?" Brian asked, raising his voice so that she could hear him.

Lila walked back into the living room. "I don't need a gun with you."

"No," he said amiably. "You don't."

Now that he was no longer staring the barrel of her service revolver, Brian looked at what Lila was wearing. The soft folds of the simple aqua dress whispered along her curves as she walked toward him.

She looked as if she hadn't gained an ounce in the last twenty years, he thought. Four children later, she still had the shape of the young woman he'd met fresh out of the academy.

Brian banked down his thoughts, allowing them to go no further. Despite her protests to the contrary, Lila was in a vulnerable place right now. Any moves he made on her now would be taking advantage of the situation—and her. That wasn't what he wanted—even if he did.

"Andrew wanted me to bring you over to his place for dinner tonight, but I thought maybe you'd prefer to start small."

"Start small?"

His mouth curved in a warm smile. "One Cavanaugh at a time."

Petting the dog, she slipped out the front door ahead of him. "You always were very intuitive."

"Part of my charm."

Lila locked the door and dropped the keys into her purse. "And your ego," she laughed.

He opened the passenger side of his car and held the door opened for her. "Oh, it's going to be like that, is it?"

She got in, aware that his glance took in her legs. Aware that she felt a stirring of pride in response. "It's going to be exactly like that."

Just like old times, Brian thought.

For a moment, it felt as if he had slipped into a time warp. And he loved it.

Chapter 5

The restaurant was known for its seafood and atmosphere. The lighting was soft and their table had a perfect view of the ocean as it flirted with the moonlight.

Brian had purposely kept the conversation light all through the entrée and main course, bringing up cases they had successfully handled during their partnership and reminiscing about old times. He'd asked her about her children and watched her face glow as she told him how Zack had made detective and that Taylor was studying to take the exam herself in a couple of months. Riley and Frank were still busy learning the ropes on the force. All were doing quite well. They took to police work like the proverbial ducks to water.

Lila confessed a bit sheepishly that she was having a little trouble coming to terms with their choice of vocation.

"Part of me wanted them to do something safer," she told him, her eyes downcast as she watched the candle light the surface of her margarita. Her lips twisted in an ironic expression. "Like join the Navy SEALS," she quipped.

As a parent, Brian understood exactly what she was saying and how she felt. But as the chief of detectives, he had found a way to come to terms with the fact that his three sons were all police detectives and his daughter was an assistant to the district attorney.

"It's not that bad," he assured her. "There are a great many more dangerous cities for a cop than Aurora."

She knew the statistics as well as anyone. Lila slowly twirled the stem of her glass between her thumb and forefinger. "There is that, I guess."

"Besides, with both their parents in law enforcement, it's not exactly a surprise that your kids chose that for themselves. It's all they've ever known—by proxy. In my family, if you take in Andrew's kids and Mike's, nine out of eleven made it into the force—and only Patience is really outside of it."

"But her husband's a cop."

Brian smiled, thinking of the way the taciturn young man had blossomed since he'd joined the family. "That he is. And so is Janelle's husband. I guess there's no getting away from it. It's in the blood."

She didn't know about that. There were those on the force whose offspring wouldn't be caught dead in a uniform. She took another sip of her drink. Despite the meal, she could feel the alcohol coursing through her veins. Making her feel somewhat light-headed. It was a struggle to remain focused on her subject.

Especially since she felt a warmth enveloping her every time she looked up at Brian.

"Some kids rebel," she pointed out. "They pick something 180 degrees different than their parents' line of work."

She took a long breath. Was that his cologne she detected? Damn, but it did things to her, made her think...

Focus, Lila, focus.

"Frank and Riley both joined the force after Ben was killed."

She didn't add that she had tried very hard to talk both her son and her daughter out of it—but both remained politely stubborn. They'd told her they understood what she was feeling, but that *they* felt that this was something they had to do. She'd more or less expected it of Riley, but Frank—Francis—was a surprise. She still thought of him as her baby.

It was hard reconciling the fact that her baby was now wearing a gun.

Brian had his own theory about why certain things evolved the way they did. "Maybe they thought that by joining, they could silence the rumors."

Lila didn't bother arguing, or pretending not to know

what he was referring to. It'd been three and a half years since Ben died and they were just now beginning to crawl out from beneath the rumors and innuendoes.

"Maybe," she allowed, taking another sip of her drink. She moved the empty glass to the side.

No time like the present, Brian thought. "About that—"

Lila looked up sharply. She'd assumed, because the subject hadn't been raised until now, that he wasn't going to say anything.

"Brian, I'd rather—"

She didn't get the chance to tell him that this was a topic she still wanted to ignore, to leave out of their little reunion. She didn't want anything spoiling this evening.

But because this was the elephant in the living room, Brian felt it needed to be acknowledged. There would be no floor space gained until this was discussed and dismissed properly. When they were partnered, they'd talked about everything and he'd felt more comfortable with her than he had with his own wife. Maybe it was selfish of him, but he wanted that back.

"Why didn't you come to me?" he asked quietly. "When this whole thing exploded, when Ben's body washed up on shore and the rumors started flying right and left, why didn't you ask my help?" When she made no answer, he added, "Or take it when I offered?"

Lila glanced out the window at the darkness outside, watching the streaks of moonlight fade into the water.

"It wasn't your problem," she told him stoically.

"That's what you say to a stranger, not a friend, not a partner."

She turned to look at him. A lot of time had passed since they'd sat in a car together, saving the world, or at least the city. A lot of changes had come about.

"Former partner."

He never thought of her that way. "I worked alone after you left the force." He shrugged. "And then the promotion came along, so as far as I'm concerned, you were the last partner I had and I always thought of you as such. In the present tense. As my partner."

The same as she, Lila thought. But she had to keep this to herself. Admitting her feelings would make him start to think. And once he did, he'd know how she felt about him. How she'd always felt, God help her.

But even if they'd had a relationship that everyone and his brother was privy to, she wouldn't have asked him to fight her battles for her. Nothing would have been won then.

"How would it have looked, my running to the chief of detectives to have him 'protect me' from the rumors, from the lies?"

Since when did she care about how things looked? One of the things he'd always admired about her was her independent streak.

"Like you were using the brains that God gave you."

But Lila shook her head. "More like I had something to hide."

And there were plenty of rumors that she'd known

about Ben being on the take, that she'd hidden the money herself or that she'd even killed Ben for the money. Horrible, horrible rumors. But she'd held her head up through it all, even offering to take a polygraph test at one point to lay the rumors to rest.

"Well," she told him firmly, "I had nothing to hide."

Her eyes were flashing. Brian placed his hand over hers, silently confirming his support. "I know that."

She squared her shoulders—but left her hand where it was.

"And I wasn't about to cower in the shadows while people tore Ben down." She couldn't bring herself to believe that he was guilty of anything except a brash temper that earned him his share of enemies. "Ben might have been a lot of things, but he wasn't a rogue cop. He wasn't any of the things they were saying. I was a cop and his wife, I would have known if he was dirty."

Brian knew she wanted him to agree, but he couldn't lie to her. Though nothing conclusive was ever proven, he felt in his bones that Ben wasn't clean. How dirty he didn't know, but not clean. Lila deserved to know his thoughts on the matter.

"Maybe the wife was blind to the cop," he suggested kindly.

He saw her set her jaw hard. "You really believe that?"

He was in a minefield and he knew it. He chose his words carefully. "I believe, when you love someone, sometimes, unconsciously, your heart has a way of fooling your brain."

The sad smile on her lips stirred a protectiveness within him. The same sort of thing that he'd felt for her years ago.

"That's when you love someone unconditionally." She shook her head, remembering things she didn't want to remember. "That wasn't Ben and me, not for a long time. My status at the police station wasn't the only thing that changed that night I got shot. Ben changed, too. He used the incident to make me stay home, saying that I owed it to the kids, that I was being selfish, risking making them motherless just because…" She shrugged, letting her voice trail off as she looked away.

"Because?" Brian prodded.

"Because he accused me of wanting to be with you." Ben had put it in far harsher terms than that, calling her a whore, but she didn't want to share that. "He was very, very jealous of you. Even jealous of the fact that you were the one who kept me alive that night." That was when she knew that she no longer loved Ben. When she realized that he would have rather she'd died than owe her life to Brian.

But there were children to consider and a part of her felt she'd somehow provoked these feelings in her husband because of the way she felt about Brian. So she'd agreed to his demands.

"So I left the force to save my marriage, and Ben was hardly home, working twice as hard to prove that he was half the man that you were." She looked down into her empty glass. The ice had dissolved, mingling with the light-colored liquid. "God help me, I never admitted this to a living soul, but the day that Ben went missing with his partner, before the police found their bodies, I'd gone to see a divorce lawyer."

Moisture formed on her eyelashes and she blinked, trying to hold back any tears. She didn't want Brian misunderstanding. Sadness had nothing to do with it.

"When they found Ben, I felt so damn guilty…" Lila pressed her lips together, trying to rein in her emotions. She looked at her empty glass and laughed shortly. "What do they put into these drinks, anyway? Truth serum?"

He'd always thought that she'd kept him away because her grief was overwhelming and turning to him would have somehow seemed disloyal to Ben because of unresolved feelings.

"Lila, if I'd known…"

She tossed her head, squaring her shoulders again. Reminding him of the stubborn stances she'd been known to take while they'd been partnered together. "Like I said, not your problem."

The hell it wasn't. "Perhaps we haven't been introduced." He put out his hand to her. "Hello, my name is Brian Cavanaugh. I care about my family *and* my friends, and I'd like to think that they'd like to have me in their corner when something bad happens to them."

Lila had had a private funeral for Ben. Although the charges against him were never proven, the cloud he'd been under when he died had never been completely cleared away, either. The department made no offer to have a public ceremony the way they did when one of their own went down in the line of duty. Brian had attended anyway, but he'd never pushed for an opportunity to talk with Lila. The look in her eyes that day had told him to keep his distance.

After that, the timing had just never seemed right. And so, the months and then years had somehow drifted away.

With a laugh, Lila took the hand he offered. "Well, I'm here now and I did come to you for help," she reminded him. "By the way, Sgt. Lopez came this morning and hooked everything up. Thank you. I feel better already."

The trace on her phone was the least he could do. It was hardly enough of a defensive measure. "And I'd feel better if you'd let me post someone at your house."

She made light of it because she just couldn't bring herself to think that she was in any real danger—which was what she knew Brian was thinking. "Why, Chief Cavanaugh, is that your subtle way of trying to get me to let you spend the night?"

His eyes met hers. He did his best to look innocent. "Thought never crossed my mind, but now that you mentioned it—"

Maybe this wasn't a road she wanted to go down, even in jest. Because it hit too close to home. "Pretend I 'unmentioned' it." She glanced at her watch. Where had the time gone? They'd been here over two hours. No wonder the waiter kept hovering and eyeing them. "I think we'd better be going. Tonight's a school night," she reminded him whimsically, referring to the fact that they both had work tomorrow. "And we both have early days tomorrow."

The waiter was at their table in less time than it took Brian to signal for him. "How do you know what I have?" he asked Lila.

She didn't bother trying to be coy. "I've kept tabs on you." Brian handed his credit card to the waiter with no hips. "I'm pretty proud of my former partner. You've done very well for yourself." She paused for a second, then added, "Susan would have been proud."

Now there she was wrong, Brian thought.

The waiter returned, presenting him with the bill.

"No, Susan would have been annoyed at the hours I keep." He signed his name after adding in a generous tip. The waiter, pretending not to look, grinned broadly. "She always complained that I was married to the job and that she was more my mistress than a wife."

"Thank you, sir," the waiter declared, then quickly removed himself.

"I hear men treat their mistresses better than their wives," Lila told him.

Something in her voice said more than her words. About to rise, he watched her closely, searching for a sign to confirm what he was thinking.

"You knew that Ben played around?"

She'd always known. Ben hadn't been that good at hiding things. Lila ran the tip of her tongue along her lips. She might have known that Brian had caught on. Nothing got by him.

"By the way you phrased that," she said, keeping her voice even, "I take it that you knew about his 'extracurricular' activities, too."

Brian didn't want to answer that, didn't want to say that he'd known and yet had never tried to warn her or give her a heads-up. He especially didn't want her to know that he'd leaned on Ben, telling the man to clean up his act or he would definitely clean it up for him. He wanted to spare her that. More than likely, Lila would tell him that it was no business of his.

So instead of answering her directly, he merely said, "You deserved better, Lila."

The corners of her mouth twitched in a half smile. The same thought had crossed her mind more than once. At other times, she felt obliged to stick it out—until she felt she couldn't take it anymore and that to stay would be the wrong thing to do. "Can't always get what you'd like."

Brian knew that for a fact. "Can't argue with that," he agreed as he rose to his feet and then held her chair for her as she did the same.

Lila turned from her front door, taking the key out of the lock and dropping it back into her purse. Butterflies took off in formation as she asked, "Would you like to come in for some coffee?"

More than you'll ever know. But the words remained unspoken.

Brian was tempted, very tempted, to take her up on her offer. To extend the evening a little longer. To walk in, close the door behind him and let things happen.

But if anything was to happen between them, it had to evolve slowly so that she wouldn't feel rushed. So that she had time to think it through and be very, very sure that she wanted to be with him.

It was up to him to set the parameters. "Much as I'd like to, it is getting late and I should let you get your rest."

As if that was possible, she thought.

She was far too keyed up to get any sleep and by some standards, the evening was still young. Not long ago she could stay up all night instead of turning in at ten.

"Just because you leave doesn't mean I'll be getting any rest." That was too honest, she chided herself silently. She gave him an alternate reason for her nocturnal vigil. "I seem to spend my nights now, waiting for the phone to ring."

He had a simple solution. "If it rings, don't pick up. Let the machine get it."

It was a matter of pride. "That would let the caller think I'm a coward."

"No, that'll show him that you're not going to play his little game. That he can't intimidate you."

That still didn't change the bottom line. "I'll still be waiting for it to ring," she confessed.

"Then shut the telephone off."

She'd thought like a mother far too long to change gears now. "What if one of the kids needs me?"

He knew that saying they were all grown up now wasn't going to carry any weight. He worried about his own and they were older than hers. "Tell them to call you on your cell."

"I'd have to give them a reason why I've stopped answering my phone."

Some of the younger detectives didn't even have a landline to begin with, claiming their cell was all they needed to stay in touch. "Say you're economizing and getting rid of your landline."

Lila frowned and shook her head. "That would be lying."

"Not if you get rid of your landline," he pointed out.

That had never even crossed her mind. Not having a working phone in the house was a completely foreign concept for her. "I forgot, you always had an answer for everything."

"No, not everything," he told her quietly. Like why he waited so long before getting together with her. Why he let so much time go by in the first place.

The porch light created an intimate setting. So much so that it became increasingly difficult to do the right thing and walk away.

He'd been doing the right thing all of his life and sometimes he grew very weary of it, of walking the straight and narrow path. Right now, he should be turning on his heel and walking toward his car, not standing here in front of her door, looking into her eyes and feeling...

Feeling.

Raising his hand to her face, Brian brushed his fingers along her cheek. Something quickened inside his gut.

Her heart felt as if it had just shifted positions, rising from her chest and into her throat, breathing was difficult and talking was a challenge.

"I had a nice time tonight, Brian." The sentence came out in a whisper.

"Me, too," he murmured.

Leaning over, he brushed his lips against her cheek. That was all he meant to do. Kiss her cheek the way he'd done a number of times before. A simple kiss between old friends.

But then she moved her head and his lips touched hers. The simple kiss blossomed into something more.

Unable to draw away, he kissed her again. Longer this time and with more feeling.

The next moment, he was taking her into his arms.

The kiss deepened, swiftly taking him beyond the scope of friendship to a place he'd never been to with her. A place he'd only touched in unguarded moments in his dreams.

Damn, but she tasted good. More than good, sensual. The pull he felt within him was almost too hard to suppress and definitely too hard to ignore.

Her pulse was racing.

All these years, she'd wondered if it would be this good. Or if kissing Brian would ultimately be a disappointment after the way she'd built it up in her mind. The chemistry she'd felt almost from the very beginning encompassed her and she leaned her body, her whole being, into this moment.

Into him.

She realized that her arms had gone around his neck and that she was standing here, acting like a teenager. And then he was drawing back. Thoughts rushed around her brain, none of them making any sense.

"I'd better go," he murmured again.

Please don't. "Are you sure you don't want to come in?"

"No, I'm not sure," he admitted. "But that's why I've got to go. We need to back away from this."

Her eyes raised to his and pinned him. "Why?"

Damned if I know. He smiled at her as he ran his knuckles against her cheek. "That's why I've got to go. To give myself time to figure out why."

"That doesn't make any sense."

"I'm working on it."

He tried to leave, he honestly did. But it was hard to walk away when his feet refused to move.

"Oh, hell."

Wrapping his arms around her, Brian brought his mouth down to hers again.

Chapter 6

The frown on his lined face deepened as the couple on the porch walked inside the house. He felt more than heard the front door click into place behind them.

He remained in the shadows, absorbing the darkness. From his vantage point, he could see the lights go on in the living room. The curtains were drawn, but he saw the silhouettes of the two people he'd watched enter the house.

And then the silhouettes retreated, moving to another part of the room—or beyond. Their outlines were no longer visible.

His imagination immediately flared, filling in what he couldn't see and a hot, bitter rage surged inside him.

His strong fingers curled into his palms, the short mani-
cured nails digging into his flesh as he unconsciously
formed fists.

There was no one to strike.

Lila hadn't felt this vibrant, this alive, in years. So
many years that she couldn't remember the last time excitement and anticipation had galloped through her like
this.

She was certain that her body temperature had risen
several degrees, enough to be identified as feverish.
But Lila couldn't measure since she was too involved
pressing her body against Brian's, seeking his warmth,
needing his heat to fuel her own.

When his hands passed over the curves of her body,
she moaned, feeling herself both melting and galvaniz-
ing at the same time. She didn't bother trying to figure
out how, she was too busy enjoying the sensations
inside of her.

"Lila." Brian whispered her name against the hol-
low of her throat. A wildness beat within her flesh, her
head spun. All she could do was hang on for dear life.
"Are you sure?"

She could hardly draw in enough breath to answer
him. "Stop asking stupid questions, Brian. I've been
sure for a very long time."

Maybe it was the margarita talking, or maybe the
margarita was giving her enough courage *to* talk. Either
way, it didn't matter. The words that had been ricochet-

ing around inside of her were finally able to see the light of day.

It was all he needed, all he wanted, the last words to make this right. Because if there was even the slightest bit of doubt lingering in her mind, Brian knew that he wouldn't be able to face himself in the morning. It wasn't about his gratification, it was about destiny.

"Where's your bedroom?" he asked hoarsely. Brian could feel her lips spreading beneath his own in a wide smile.

How so like Brian, she thought. He was always mindful of doing the right thing. If he hadn't been, then maybe he would have never taken no as an answer when he'd come by with his offer to help right after Ben's body was found.

And she wouldn't have been alone all this time.

"No one lives here anymore, Brian. We can make love on the stairs if we want to."

"No stairs." Brian framed her face in his hands. Part of her was still unable to believe that after all this time, this was finally happening. "I want to do this the right way."

"Any way you do it will be right," she told him, her breath growing shorter. And then, because he was waiting, she added, "First door to your right at the top of the stairs."

He kissed her lips again, just to be sure, and tasted her eagerness. Nothing had ever felt so right before. Picking her up into his arms, he sealed his lips to hers and took the first step toward the staircase.

Behind them, in the foyer, the front door opened and then closed again, the sound reverberating through the room.

"Hey, Mom, whose car is in the driveway?"

Brian barely had enough time to set Lila back down before her oldest son, Zack, walked out of the living room and into the hallway. And saw them. But as to what he thought was anyone's guess. Zack had a fantastic poker face.

"Oh. Chief, I didn't realize that you were here with Mom—is something wrong?" Zack's deep blue eyes darted back and forth from his mother to the chief of detectives, a vague confusion wrinkling his smooth forehead. And then what he had walked in on apparently dawned on him. "Did I…interrupt something?"

Brian rallied first. He'd always been quick on his feet, but that speed usually involved some sort of police-related situation, not a personal one.

"No," he told the young detective, carefully edging away from Lila, "your mother and I were just catching up on old times." His eyes shifted to Lila's face. "And I was just leaving." He took her hand between both of his. "It was wonderful seeing you again, Lila." An idea suddenly came to him. "Andrew's having a family barbecue in a few weeks. Why don't you, Zack—" he looked toward the detective "—and the rest of your kids come? The more, the merrier." He was pretty certain that Andrew had that tattooed on his person somewhere.

"But you just said it was a family barbecue," Lila protested. She was fairly surprised that her knees had come around so quickly. They'd all but been melted a moment ago.

"That's right—and to Andrew, anyone on the force is considered family." His eyes shifted to Zack. "Think about it." He nodded at Lila. "I'll see myself out."

She wasn't about to let him just slip away like smoke, not after he'd nearly caused her to burn up.

"No, let me walk you to the door," she insisted. "It's the least I can do since you paid for dinner." With that, she took Brian's arm and ushered him back to the front door.

She held her peace until they were at the door. Opening it, she let him go out first, then joined him on the front step.

"I'm sorry about this. They all have keys to the house," she confessed. As each moved out, she'd insisted that they keep a copy in case of emergency—and to know that they always could come home. "But they don't usually drop in during the week."

He couldn't deny that he felt frustrated, but he could see an upside to this. "Maybe it's just as well. Some things only become sweeter if you have to wait for them."

Her eyes held his for a long moment. "I think we've both been waiting for a very long time."

This time, when he brushed a kiss against her cheek, he backed away before the steel trap of temptation closed around him.

"A little longer won't hurt," he assured her before turning toward his car.

Wrapping her arms around herself, Lila watched Brian get into his car and then drive away.

A little longer.

That meant that this wasn't over. That maybe this was just the beginning. The very thought made her pulse race again. It was nice to know some things didn't necessarily change with time. She felt like a teenager again.

Closing the door behind her, she was face-to-face with her son.

Zack's eyes searched her face. "I *did* interrupt something, didn't I?"

Lila didn't answer immediately. She'd always made it a point not to lie to her children. If she was guilty of anything in that department, it was the sin of omission. *Not* telling them things. But that was only to protect them from what they were better off not knowing.

Like how verbally abusive their father had become toward the end. She wanted them to draw their own conclusions about their father and not see Ben through her eyes but their own. For her part, she'd become completely and devastatingly disenchanted with the man she had once loved with all her young heart.

She shrugged carelessly now in response to Zack's question. "Just some conversation, that's all."

The enigmatic smile on his lips told her that he knew better. "Give me a little credit, Mom. Your face was flushed."

She had that covered. "It's warm in here."

"Not that warm," he countered. "And you looked guilty, like the time when you went back to work without telling Dad." He saw her open her mouth to defend her actions and he raised his hands to fend off the flow of words. "Hey, Mom, it's okay. You have a right to live your life. You're not some Hindu widow expected to throw herself on the funeral pyre just because her husband's dead."

"That practice went out of style a long time ago," she informed him.

"You know what I mean." Making himself at home, he headed toward the refrigerator and took out one of the bottles of beer his mother always kept on tap for him and his brother. "I like the chief," he told her heartily. "Always have. He's fair and honest, and he doesn't play favorites even though he could. Hell, most of his family's on the force in some capacity or other and he could be handing out commendations right and left if he wanted to. But he doesn't."

Turning from the refrigerator, Zack jerked off the cap with his thumb, sending the metallic cap flying onto the countertop. He took a long swig before saying, "Riley, Frank and Taylor have been worried about you."

"Riley, Frank and Taylor, but not you."

He pretended to shrug noncommittally. "Me maybe a little."

Lila looked at her oldest born. What had brought this on? Had he found out about the phone calls in the middle of the night? But how? Brian was the only one she'd told and he had in turn told Lopez and sworn him to secrecy.

"Why? What brought on this sudden concern?"

"Because you're alone and you shouldn't be. You've still got a lot to offer."

Only the very young could phrase it that way to someone who *didn't* have one foot in the grave. Her mouth curved wryly. "Thank you for that."

Zack walked back into the living room. "You know what I mean." He nodded toward the closed door. "If you want to start seeing the chief, I think it's great."

Poor Zack, she thought, he meant well. But this wasn't something she was willing to have up for discussion just yet. Because she had no idea where it was going.

For a second there, just before Zack came along, she'd been set to go, to tumble into bed with Brian and feel all those things a woman was supposed to feel. But now that her blood was cooling, well, maybe Zack's untimely entrance had saved her from herself.

Everything happened for a reason.

But right now there were some ground rules she needed to refresh. "Not that I'm 'seeing' the chief, but if I were, I wouldn't have to ask any of you for permission."

Zack's eyes raised to hers. She saw amusement in them. "I know that. I also know that you'd feel better about it if we were happy you were seeing someone."

There was no denying that he was right, that if she

felt that Zack or any of the others took exception to her seeing Brian, or anyone else for that matter, it would make her hesitate and reevaluate her actions. Their peace of mind meant the world to her.

She affectionately touched her son's face. "How did you get to be so smart?"

With a laugh, Zack kissed the top of her head. "I had a great teacher. Strict, but fair."

Ben always said she was a pushover when it came to the kids. One of the rare times when he was right. "I was never strict."

Sitting down on the sofa, Zack made himself comfortable. He rested his boot-clad feet on the coffee table. "I thought you were when I was younger."

Lila pushed his feet off again. She didn't need him scuffing up her furniture. "And now?"

He grinned and a dimple winked at the side of his mouth. "Now I don't know why you didn't hit me upside the head back then—a lot."

As he began to move his feet back onto the table, Lila pretended to raise her hand to strike and deadpanned, "Never too late."

The feet remained on the floor. Zack took the hand she raised and kissed her knuckles. "I could always tell when you were bluffing."

Just then, Lila heard the front door being unlocked and opening again. She spared Zack a quizzical glance and then looked in the direction of the front door. "Are you expecting someone?" she asked.

Before he could respond, she had her answer.

"Hi, Mom," Riley's and Taylor's voices blended together as they walked into the living room practically simultaneously.

They were followed by the youngest of the brood. Frank nodded his head at her. "Mom."

Something was definitely up. They just didn't all just "happen" to congregate at the house without a mandated invitation.

Lila looked from one young face to another. The girls, willowy and slender, had her coloring while Zack and Frank were dark, like Ben. But no one ever missed the fact that they were all related.

"Okay, to what do I owe this impromptu gathering of the clan?" she asked.

Riley took the lead. "*Dirty Harry* is on tonight." She mentioned the cable station and then glanced at her watch. "Starts in five minutes. We thought you might want to watch it for the—" Stopping, she turned toward her sister. "How many does this make, Taylor?"

"Twenty-seventh, twenty-eighth time," her older sister guesstimated, rolling her eyes. But the expression on her face was pure affection.

"We thought it'd been a while since we all got together," Zack added. Frank nodded in agreement.

Lila's eyes swept over her brood. In her mind's eye, she could still see them as little children, running around, yelling and fairly bouncing off the walls—or each other. But those days were gone. It had been years since any of them had been shorter than she was. Now, to varying degrees, they all towered over her. They got their stature from their father. Their sense of honor, thank God, they got from her.

"Am I dying?" Her expression was somber as she looked from one to another.

"Don't exaggerate, Mom," Riley chided. "We show up here. Occasionally," she tagged on, anticipating her mother's response.

"Not *en masse*," Lila pointed out. "You only do that at Thanksgiving and Christmas—and certain birthdays if I threaten you with bodily harm."

"And now we show up for Clint Eastwood movies," Zack told her. He turned on the set and then draped both arms over the back of the sofa, making himself even more comfortable.

Frank was already on his way to the kitchen. "Got any chips?" he asked, his voice drifting back to them.

Since they'd moved out, she made it a point not to have too much junk food around. The temptation to eat it was hard to resist. She only stocked up when she knew one of them might be dropping by.

"I'm afraid I'm fresh out of chips," Lila confessed. "But I have beer."

"Have no fear," Riley announced, pulling a small yellow package out of what Zack maintained was the largest purse on the North American continent. "I brought popcorn." She grinned at her mother. "What's a Clint Eastwood movie without popcorn?"

"Stop talking and start popping," Frank ordered, pointing toward the microwave oven standing on the kitchen counter.

Riley narrowed her eyes at the youngest member of the family. Frank was easily the tallest of them. "Watch who you're ordering around, baby brother."

"Watch that baby stuff," he countered without missing a beat. "You're only eleven and a half months older than me."

Riley chucked Frank under the chin, something she knew annoyed him. "And don't you forget it, *Francis*," she deliberately drew out his given name, then glanced over her shoulder at her mother just before she went into the kitchen to place the kernel-filled bag into the microwave. "Honestly, Mom, I don't know how you put up with these others."

There was a lot of love here, Lila thought, scanning the room. She saw Frank slide bonelessly into a chair beside the sofa. "Just lucky, I suppose."

Lila turned toward Zack, knowing that he was the one who most likely organized this gathering. She and her oldest were always a little bit more in sync than the others. More than anyone, he knew how to get to her and what made her happy. Beneath his dark good looks and his steely exterior, he was a sensitive boy.

Man, she silently corrected herself. At twenty-six, Zack Anthony McIntyre was a man—even though, on occasion, she still thought of him as her little boy. The little boy who, at the age of ten, had thrown himself in front of her to protect her from Ben when his anger was getting the better of him. He would have wound up striking Zack had she not pulled the boy back. To his credit, Ben had stormed out of the house, cursing, rather than allowing the situation to escalate.

Over the years Zack never said a word against his father, but of all of them, he was the one who really knew what Ben could be like.

He'd grown up too fast, she thought now. She wished she could give him those years back. Those years when he should have been a happy-go-lucky little boy instead of a little man, burdened with things he shouldn't have even known about.

She crossed over to the sofa.

"What channel did you say *Dirty Harry* was on?" Lila asked Zack, nodding toward the forty-inch plasma TV that he and his siblings had given her as a Christmas present last year.

He paused to think for a second. "I think it's channel sixty-one."

Lila glanced at the TV screen. The upper right-hand corner said that the set was currently on channel seven. Then eight. Then nine. Zack was pressing the up arrow on the remote control's channel selector.

A typical male move, she thought.

"Why don't you just punch in sixty-one?" she suggested.

But Zack merely grinned at her as the channels continued to zip by one at a time. "I like doing it my way."

Taylor huffed as she bounced down beside him on the sofa.

"Mind like a steel trap," she complained. Then, lest he miss her meaning, added, "Rusted shut." Pretending she wasn't there, Zack went on going through the channels one by one. Rolling her eyes, Taylor put out her hand. "Give me that," she demanded.

Zack ignored her outstretched hand. "Never come between a man and his remote control."

Her green eyes darting toward her mother, Taylor had the good grace to swallow the name she was going to call him.

"Popcorn's ready," Riley announced, carrying a huge blue bowl into the room.

"About time," Frank told her.

"Keep it down, the movie's starting," Zack said needlessly.

Ben'd had more than his share of faults, Lila thought as she took her seat beside Taylor, but he had given her four wonderful children. That alone absolved him of a multitude of sins.

Chapter 7

She dreamed of him that night.

Not of Brian, even though she'd fallen asleep thinking about him, but of Ben. The dream was so real, she could feel herself breaking out into a weakening, cold sweat.

Lila felt a presence hovering over her in the bedroom. Ben.

Lost in the depths of sleep, her heart hammering, she struggled to pry open her eyes. She failed several times. Each lid felt glued shut, impossible to lift. Even though she was dreaming, Lila knew, just knew, that if she could only open her eyes, could only look around, she'd see she was alone. And then her heart would stop hammering.

Finally, after what seemed like eternity, she managed to open her eyes. The sound of heavy breathing accosted her, making her heart jump again.

It was only after a few moments had passed that she realized there was no one standing over her, that the heavy breathing she heard was coming from her. Still, she couldn't shake the feeling that someone had been in the room with her. That their essence still lingered, clinging to every surface in her bedroom.

Turning on the lamp revealed no one standing in the shadows or taking shelter behind her drapes.

She was alone. And maybe going a little crazy.

Duchess was on the floor beside her bed. The dog raised her head as if to ask, "Why d'you put the light on?"

The aging German shepherd appeared completely at ease and, after a beat, Duchess put her head down again. If there'd been an intruder, Duchess would have barked. She barked at the mail carrier each time a new one showed up on the doorstep. Duchess was leery of strangers until she became used to them.

The dog would have barked if someone had slipped into the bedroom. Right?

Lila sat up, feeling wide awake and exhausted at the same time. Her head ached as thoughts scrambled about her brain. Duchess wouldn't have barked at someone she knew.

Someone like Ben.

"Stop it, Ben's dead," Lila upbraided herself. "You

buried him so he damn well better have been dead at the time."

But she couldn't free herself of the feeling that someone had been watching her. That someone had been here, in the house, after the movie had ended and Zack, Taylor, Riley and Frank had all kissed her and gone their separate ways.

"Some police officer you are," she jeered out loud, "seeing ghosts in the shadows."

Lila took a long breath, trying to steady her nerves. Trying to calm down.

She'd almost succeeded when she saw it.

A leaf beneath the windowsill.

A lone leaf highlighted against the light gray rug. Dropped by someone coming in? By someone leaving?

Most likely, she silently insisted, it was just a leaf that had clung to Duchess's coat when she'd taken one of her numerous runs into the backyard. It just so happened that the leaf had fallen off in the middle of the night.

Made sense, right?

But sense or not, an uneasiness continued to spread through her.

She was about to turn off the light again when the phone rang. Lila stifled a scream as her heart launched itself into triple-time. She stared at the telephone accusingly when it rang again.

Brian had told her to let the machine pick up any calls, but she couldn't bring herself to just sit here, waiting for the phone to ring three more times before the answering machine switched on.

Making the decision to end this once and for all, Lila yanked the receiver up and held it against her ear. "Look, you sick, perverted scum, you keep this up and I'm going to track you down and trust me, you *really* don't want me to do that."

"Oh, I don't know, it sounds promising," the deep male voice on the other end said. "What do you intend to do after you track me down?"

Lila was stunned speechless. Almost. "Brian?" she asked uncertainly. It was eleven-thirty at night, what was he doing calling so late?

As if he'd just heard her thoughts, he said, "Yes. Sorry if I'm calling so late but I wanted to check in on you." He paused for a second, as if trying to decide how to word what he was about to say. "And to ask if you had any trouble with Zack." He hadn't called any earlier because he thought Zack might still be there and he didn't want Lila catching any grief over his expression of concern.

Her mind summoning the movie they'd all just watched, she didn't understand what Brian was referring to. "Trouble?"

"You know, with his walking in on us like that…" His voice trailed off.

She had no idea why, but Brian's concern about the impression he might have made on her son seemed sweet somehow. He obviously cared what her family thought. Relieved that it was Brian on the other end of the line and not her night caller, she let the sound of his voice fill the room. It comforted her.

Scooting back on the bed, she leaned against the headboard. "On the contrary," she laughed. "He's given his permission."

It was Brian's turn not to follow. "Excuse me?"

"His permission," she repeated. "For us to see one another. Zack seemed to think that he walked in on a date."

Permission, huh? It had been a long time since he'd felt the need to obtain permission to see someone. The thought made him smile. It was absolutely true. The more things changed, the more they actually stayed the same. "Well, he did."

"We were just catching up on old times," she protested, choosing not to think about the kiss and where it might have led if Zack hadn't walked into the house just then—or if he'd walked in ten minutes later.

Lila banked down her thoughts. She *definitely* did not want to go there.

She heard him laugh. "I'm not sure if you know this, but you can do that on a date. Catch up," he added in case she'd lost track of the point.

She pretended not to hear him. "And I was asking for your help."

"Ditto, see above."

Giving up, Lila laughed. Duchess moved over closer to her and raised her head to be scratched. Lila obliged. "Have it your way."

"Now there's something I never tire of hearing," Brian said. The pause that followed seemed to drag itself out. "Lila, is there anything wrong?"

"No."

She'd answered that too quickly, she thought. And Brian had always been good about picking up on tones and reading in between the lines.

The next moment he proved her right because he asked, "But?"

Sighing, she dragged her hand through her hair. If she told him about her dream, about the leaf, he was going to think she was behaving like some addle-brained woman afraid of her own shadow.

"It's nothing."

He wasn't accepting excuses. "Let me be the judge of that."

Taking a breath, she dove in. "All right. After the kids left—" She was getting ahead of herself, she realized. "Zack wasn't the only one who came over, the others came after you went home. Anyway, after they left and I went to bed, I fell asleep. I woke up when it felt like there was someone else in the house, in my room." Damn, that sounded so lame. "I guess I was just having a bad dream."

But Brian wasn't so quick to dismiss her feeling. "Are you sure?"

"Yes." She licked her lower lip. "No." And then she sighed again. "Maybe."

"Well, I think that covers the entire spectrum," he told her philosophically. "I'll be right over."

Guilt immediately jumped onto center stage. "I didn't mean for you to come over."

"I outrank you, Lila," he informed her. "I'm coming over." And then he gave her another option. "Unless you want to call one of your kids and have them come over instead."

They'd already covered that when she'd came to his office to tell him about the phone calls. "I don't want them worrying about me and I definitely don't want them to think their mother is losing her mind."

"Then it's settled," he said with finality. "I'm coming over. I can be there in twenty minutes."

"This isn't necessary."

But she was making her protest to a dial tone.

Brian wasn't over in twenty minutes, he was over in fourteen.

Lila opened the door the moment he placed his thumb on the doorbell. "You got here fast."

He tried not to notice that she wore a black silk robe, or that the sides seemed to drift apart with every word she uttered. He waited for her to step to the side. When she did, the robe slipped a little farther apart. The nightgown beneath wasn't nearly thick enough.

"One of the perks of being the chief of detectives," he said as he walked in. "I get to use the siren when I need to."

She closed the door behind him. "I feel guilty having you come over."

"Don't," he told her, turning around to face her. He deliberately focused on her eyes. "You didn't ask, I offered, remember? Besides, I wasn't sleeping anyway."

"But you said you had an early morning," she reminded him.

"Meetings can be rearranged." Her peace of mind came first. Now that she had finally sought him out, he wasn't about to be cavalier about it. Walking into the living room, he crossed to the sofa and sat down. "You can go back to bed."

He seemed to be settling in for the duration. "And you're going to—what, spend the night just sitting there?"

He smiled as he nodded. "That's the plan."

She wasn't a child. She didn't have to have her hand held. Imposing like this on Brian was wrong. "I tell you what, you can watch me double-check the locks on the doors and windows and then you can go home."

His eyes met hers. His were smiling. "Better idea, I'll watch you double-check the locks on the doors and windows and then you go to bed while I take the couch. Think of it as just another stakeout, except more comfortable."

"That was ten years ago."

"Eight," he corrected her. He remembered, to the day, when she first left the force.

"Eight," she echoed. "That's still a long time ago."

Age wasn't something he dwelled on. He still

thought of himself as being thirty-two. He still logged in time at the gym whenever he got the chance. "Not much has changed."

The years had been kind to him, she thought fondly. But they had still gone by. "Except time."

Brian arched an eyebrow. "Are you trying to tell me that I'm getting old?"

Lila laughed. "No, never that." And then she sighed, sitting down beside him. Her robe parted even further. With a swift movement, she drew the two sides back together. "This is my fault. I should have never said anything to you when you called."

"I would have known anyway."

Something skittered through her. Being here like this with him, in her home, alone except for the dog, seemed suddenly extremely intimate to her. She was acutely aware that she was nude beneath the robe and night-gown.

Her breath grew a little shorter but she did her best to sound flippant. "Oh, you've added mind-reading to your list of abilities?"

"Not mind-reading, just being in-tuned to certain people." There was a time when he'd thought of them as being two halves of a whole. They'd worked well together, anticipating one another. Acting in concert. "You and I worked very closely for over six years. I got to know the way you thought—just like you got to know how I thought."

She couldn't take her eyes off his. Lila felt a hypnotic

pull inside her gut. Why was the air suddenly standing still around her?

"Meaning?"

Had she really forgotten how close they'd been? He couldn't bring himself to believe that. "You knew that if you said that you thought someone had gotten into the house—even if you dismissed it the next moment as your imagination—I'd come over on the chance that it was actually true."

"No, I—" The denial faded from her lips. Her face flushed slightly as she shrugged. The silk robe slid off her shoulder and she tugged it back into place. "All right," she admitted. "Maybe, in a moment of weakness, I did. But I'm sorry now." Lila glanced away. "I guess I'm not as fearless as I used to be."

He saw how hard that was for her to admit. Very gently, his fingers beneath her chin, he turned her head so that she was looking at him again. "That's a shame. I really liked that fearless girl."

Lila laughed shortly, shaking her head. "I haven't been a girl in a very long time."

"I disagree." His smile seemed to go straight to her stomach and havoc ensued. "To me, you'll always be a girl."

It felt as if his eyes were touching her. Breathing was becoming tricky. "Brian?"

His name was barely a whisper on her lips. Why did that excite him so? "Yes?"

It seemed like an effort to get each word out. "Just

how long are you going to keep talking before you kiss me?"

He framed her face with his hands. "I think I've just run out of things to say."

"Good."

The last word vibrated against her lips as Brian brought his mouth down to hers. Instantly he felt his body responding, aching, wanting her with a fierceness that was all but overwhelming.

But reason still prevailed and with a great deal of reluctance, he forced himself to draw his head back instead of deepening the kiss. "I'm not going to be much of a bodyguard if I'm going to be this close to your body."

If he stopped now, she was going to self-destruct, she just knew it. "I don't need someone guarding my body," Lila told him.

To underscore her statement, Lila nipped his lower lip with her teeth, then slid the tip of her tongue along it. His sharp intake of breath told her that she was driving him just as crazy.

Placing her hand over his, she guided it to her breast. Something wild began beating in her chest.

Her voice was low, thick, as she said, "I need this far more."

Brian gave up trying to resist, gave up trying to convince himself that he was strong enough to walk away this time, the way he had shut down his surging desire all those other times.

"Not half as much as I do."

She didn't know if it was the words or the sound of his raspy voice, or both, that brought her up to a level of excitement she hadn't thought possible.

Afraid that this would end at any moment, unable to rein herself in any longer, Lila tugged on his clothes. She urgently pulled his sweater over his head, carelessly tossing it aside. With feverish hands she worked at his belt, unnotching it and then pulling it out of its loops in a sweeping movement that would have made a bull whip expert proud.

And all the while, as she stripped him, she spread a flurry of quick, sensual kisses along his face, his neck, his shoulders, frantic to divest him of all the obstacles and to feel his flesh against hers.

She shivered, not from the cold, but from anticipation. His hands were everywhere, mimicking her movements.

"Not fair," she complained as Brian took off first her dark silk robe, then the nightgown that was lighter than air. "You have more clothes."

"Not for long." Rising, his hands bracketed on her arms and taking her up with him, Brian kicked off the jeans she'd guided down his hips with fingers that weren't quite steady just moments ago.

This time, he didn't ask about her bedroom. This time, there was little occasion for words or residual hesitation. He'd never been so sure of anything in his life, sure that this was right, that it was meant to happen and just as sure that if it stopped, he'd implode.

Without her clothes Lila was even more beautiful, more sensual. Brian discovered that her clothing didn't hide a multitude of flaws, it merely hid her. Hid her perfection.

As if to assure himself that he wasn't just imagining all this, Brian ran the palms of his hands all along her body, dipping into the curves, cupping the swells. Committing everything to memory through the sensation of touch. Touch and taste.

She all but set him on fire.

Brian pressed her against the sofa, his body looming over hers. But rather than take her the way he so sorely wanted to, he reined in his desire and slowly took his time. Began to familiarize himself with every inch of her as it lay exposed to his view.

"How do you do it?" he marveled. "How do you look like this after all these years?"

She was so relieved that he wasn't disappointed, she was almost giddy. "You don't have to sweet talk me, Brian," she told him, thrilling to his caress and to the promise of what was to come. "In case you haven't noticed—" she wiggled in beneath him, watching desire flare in his eyes "—you've already won me over."

"No sweet talk," he told her, his breath, like hers, growing shorter. "Just the facts, ma'am. Just the facts." It was a line from a classic police drama they'd discovered, years ago, that they both liked as kids.

He brought his mouth down on her belly, curving his tongue along her skin. When he felt her quiver beneath him, there were no words to describe the reaction that coursed through his veins, that urged him to continue. He couldn't get enough of her.

It was perfect.

More than perfect. Just as she had always thought, hoped, fantasized it would be. She felt herself trapped between ecstasy and the desire for fulfillment. Brian did things to her with such exquisite movements, she could barely breathe.

Joy filled her even as she ached for more.

All sorts of emotions, sensations, collided within her. It was like having lightning coursing through her veins. Lightning and explosions. Beautiful, colorful explosions.

She had never felt this sort of sweet agony before. The swift movements of his mouth and tongue brought her to one climax after another. Something she'd never felt in all her years of marriage.

Ben had tried to be a good lover, but it was by rote, as if he were doing it by the numbers, in a given way every single time. Nothing ever changed. He never had a desire to try anything new.

But this was all new. Including her being breathless even before they came together for the final joining. There wasn't a part of her that Brian hadn't played, hadn't touched and primed. By the time he finally drew his body up along hers and then entered her, Lila felt almost rabid with passion.

She raised her hips, meeting him partway and then,

as they began to move in one all-encompassing rhythm, they rushed off together to the ultimate summit. Her mouth sealed to his, she cried out his name as she sailed over the top.

Chapter 8

The euphoria that came in the wake of their lovemaking settled into a pleasant glow. Lila savored it for a few moments before she finally opened her eyes.

She was tucked against Brian, with the sofa at her back. Duchess was off to the side, her eyes closed, in that semidozing state that dogs assume.

Everything felt absolutely wonderful. Especially her. Contentment poured through her veins like warmed honey.

"That," she said when her heart finally ceased tap-dancing in her throat, "was a long time in coming."

Brian brushed a hair from her cheek, allowing his

fingers to linger a little while against her skin. "The best things in life are worth waiting for."

God, this felt so right, being here with him like this. She expected to feel guilt, remorse, possibly disappointment. Instead she wanted to embrace the whole world in a giant bear hug.

Or at the very least, to climb up on her roof and shout for joy.

She settled for snuggling against Brian and feeling like a kid again. "I thought the best things in life were free."

"That, too." She watched his smile grow. His breath caressed her skin when he spoke. "I don't plan on charging you for this."

"Nice to know." She drew in a deep breath, and took in his scent, a combination of aftershave, soap and just the slightest hint of the sweat he had worked up. She could feel her pulse accelerate again, could feel a pull from deep within her abdomen.

"I think—" she trailed her fingertip along his cheekbone the way she'd always longed to do when they were riding together, "—if you're planning on spending the night, you should sleep in my bed upstairs."

He feigned surprise. "Why, Detective McIntyre, are you propositioning me?"

A laugh escaped her lips. "I think we're a little past that."

"No," he told her quietly just before he cupped her cheek and kissed her again. "We're never past that."

The gleam in his eyes was hard to ignore. "Are you trying to tell me you could do this again?" Even as she asked, she felt the answer to her question hardening against her.

He read her thoughts and made no effort to bank down his. "Why is that so hard to believe?"

There'd only been two men in her life, Ben and now Brian. She could only draw on what she knew. "Isn't this the part where you roll over on your side and go to sleep?"

Brian kissed her shoulder, creating a labyrinth of sensations that went off like Fourth of July sparklers.

"Clearly," he teased, "there are sections of your education that are badly in need of updating."

"I guess you have your work cut out for you." She grinned, rising. "Well, I'm always willing to learn." Reaching for her robe, Lila began to slip it on.

But Brian stopped her, sliding it off her shoulders again.

"Don't bother putting it on," he told her, letting it fall back to the floor. He slipped his arm around her and pulled her to him. "I'm only going to take it off you again."

When had she ever felt this giddy, this carefree? "Pulling rank again?"

"If I have to." He paused for just a moment to kiss her again before urging her toward the stairs. "Among other things," he added.

It was all she could do to keep from melting into him again. "All those years of riding around beside you, I never knew you were a love machine."

"Life is a constant learning process," he told her as they began to climb the stairs.

Heaven knew she wasn't about to argue with that.

He stepped out of the shadows, still watching the house, as he had been for the duration of the evening. Briefly he considered going back into the yard. The gate was still open after he'd picked the lock. He was going to have to fix that before morning.

But right now, his anger rose in his throat like hot bile. It colored everything he saw and would impede his actions. In this state, he was prone to making a mistake.

Just as Lila had made hers.

Jared popped his head into his father's office on the off chance of finding him in. This was his third try.

It was always a fifty-fifty chance that the room would be empty. Everyone, especially the family, knew that Brian Cavanaugh believed in being a hands-on chief of d's. That meant making the rounds of the different departments he was responsible for, getting to know his detectives and their methods of operating. He'd stand back and silently listen to their interrogations, read through their reports and talk to them as equals. Most of the force hoped that he would never retire.

Jared was gratified to find him in this morning. And surprised to see his father's chair turned away from his desk, facing the window. The former was piled high with the contents of the two boxes that Brian had brought to him from the basement.

For a second Jared debated slipping away again. His father obviously had a lot on his mind. But the internal debate was terminated the next moment as his father turned toward him.

"Jared, what are you doing here?" Even as he greeted his son, things began to click into place in his mind. This was serendipity, Brian thought.

His hand in his coat pocket, Jared fingered the tickets he had come about. The expression on his father's face distracted him for a second. He seemed different somehow. The conversation he'd had this morning at breakfast with Uncle Andrew came back to him.

Crossing the threshold, Jared smiled. "Hi, you got a minute?"

"For you, always." They weren't just empty words. Jared knew his father, possibly the busiest man in Aurora, sincerely meant them. "What's on your mind?"

"I've got baseball tickets to a game tomorrow. The A's are playing. First game of a three-game series," he added. The Oakland A's were his father's favorite team. Going to baseball games had been a family ritual when they were kids. "I thought that maybe you'd like to come with me."

Brian had been poring over the files on his desk all morning and there was a headache building behind his eyes. Someday soon he was going to have to break down and finally get reading glasses.

Leaning back in his chair now, he laced his fingers behind his head.

"Why isn't Maren going with you?"

Jared produced the tickets, placing them on top of a closed folder on the desk.

"I didn't ask her." He didn't mention that right now his wife was too busy fighting overwhelming nausea to go anywhere. "She can't see the point of grown men getting paid a fortune for hitting a ball with a little stick." He shrugged off the sentiment. "Besides, I thought it'd been a while since you and I did anything together and I know how much you like the A's. It's not that far away and I'll drive," he offered in case his father saw that as a problem.

"Thanks, I appreciate it, but I'm going to have to pass." Because he enjoyed the company of all his kids, he hated saying no. "I'm going to be busy."

"Burning the midnight oil here?" Jared guessed, nodding at the boxes.

"No." He'd been spending a good deal of his off hours with Lila for the past couple of weeks. He'd been to her place and had her over to his. It amazed him how much warmth and light she brought into his house. It no longer felt cold or empty the way it had ever since Janelle had gotten married.

His father was turning down spending time with a family member and it wasn't because of the demands of his work. Curious, Jared studied his father's face for a moment. There was something in his father's eyes, a gleam that he hadn't seen in quite some time.

A grin split Jared's face as it suddenly lit up. "Uncle Andrew was right, there is a spring to your step."

Brian eyed him. "In case you haven't noticed, I happen to be sitting down. Don't make me doubt your powers of observation, Detective."

"You know what I mean."

Brian assumed the face of complete innocence. "Haven't the slightest."

Jared cocked his head, his eyes narrowing. Only one thing he knew of that made a man look like that. "You seeing somebody?"

"I see lots of people every day. It's part of my job."

Jared slipped the tickets into his pocket. "I think you have this backward. Kids are supposed to be evasive with their parents, not the other way around."

"'Kids,'" Brian pointed out, "aren't supposed to give their parents the third degree."

Jared crossed his arms before him and leaned against the wall, still studying his father. "This isn't even a first degree, it's a casual question. You've just turned down free tickets to a baseball game. You're going to be busy, but not with police work—"

The excuse he'd given himself for seeing her as much as he was, was that he was looking into Lila's mysterious caller. "That's not entirely true."

That brought Jared up short. "Then it does involve police work?"

Brian spread his hands, unwilling to explain any further. "In a way."

A little of the impatience they shared surfaced within Jared. "Are you going to tell me or do I have to guess?"

Brian glanced toward the folder he'd been looking at earlier. The silent debate in his head took a new turn. "I'm the chief of detectives, you don't get to guess. But you do get to do something for me."

Jared stopped leaning and moved forward. "I'm listening."

"I'm looking into an old homicide."

That would explain the boxes and the folders everywhere. Jared nodded toward the one closest to him. "A cold case?"

Brian had never cared for the generic label. "Lukewarm." When Jared looked amused, he added, "It's only three and a half years old."

"What's so special about it?" It would have to be special in order to get his father to personally dig into it when there were fresh cases on the books for him to oversee.

The word "special" didn't seem to fit, at least not as far as he was concerned. Heinous was more like it, since it involved a cop killing. "Ben McIntyre and his partner, Dean Walker, were found murdered on the beach within two days of one another. Everyone just assumed that someone from the drug cartel did it, but they never found anyone actually guilty."

It was hard having something like that on the record. Despite his own workload, Jared was willing to pitch in. "What do you want me to do?"

"I'd like you to nose around a bit—off the record." He felt that was important. If Ben had been a dirty cop, he might have had other "partners" than the one who'd been killed with him. There was no sense in alerting anyone at this stage. "See if anyone's heard someone bragging about 'getting away with' a double cop killing." In his experience, bragging rights were all part of the game. "You know, a friend of a friend who has a friend who heard so-and-so say he killed a couple of cops on the take, that kind of thing."

Jared narrowed his eyes. "You're looking for hearsay?"

That wasn't his first choice but you took what you could. "You have to start somewhere," Brian told him with a shrug. "At this point, I'm looking for anything that'll give me a clue. See if you can get Troy and Callie to help you," he suggested, naming both his son and his oldest niece.

"McIntyre," Jared repeated, looking at his father. And then it dawned on him. "Wasn't that the name of your old partner? Lila?" One thought led to another. "Ben McIntyre, the vice cop, that was her husband, right?" Brian nodded. "Why are you looking into this now—or is that one of the questions I'm not supposed to be asking?"

Brian began moving the stacks of paper around, searching for the file he wanted to give Jared so he could familiarize himself with the case. He'd just seen it a few minutes ago.

"For future reference, you're never supposed to question the chief of d's." He glance up at Jared. "But you can ask," he told him magnanimously. "I'm looking into it because Lila McIntyre called me a couple of weeks ago." He debated leaving it at that, then decided that Jared needed a little more information. "She's been getting strange phone calls in the middle of the night. Could be nothing, could be something. Could be tied to Ben's murder. I don't know but I thought I'd have some of my best people poke around, see what they come up with. Sometimes fresh eyes can see things the way weather-beaten detectives can't…" Brian's voiced trail off.

His interest was piqued already. "You don't have to use flattery."

"I'm not," Brian said simply. "If you weren't good, I'd let you know."

Jared nodded, knowing that his father would find a way to temper any criticism. He wasn't the type just to tear someone apart "for their own good." More than most, Brian Cavanaugh was a people person. "So is Lila the reason you're standing me up?"

Brian spared his oldest a warning glance. "I'd use my investigative powers elsewhere if I were you, Detective Cavanaugh."

Jared grinned. "Sorry, it doesn't always work that way. Just so you know, I think Lila McIntyre's a neat lady. She used to give me gummy bears when you two were partners."

"Gummy bears," Brian echoed, shaking his head. Lila always had a supply of them with her. He'd just assumed she'd picked them up for her own kids whenever she got the chance. "Is that how you measure people's worth?"

The humor in Jared's eyes was hard to miss. "Among other things."

"I should pass that on to Maren. Here, I want you to go through this. Highlights of the case," Brian added as he unearthed the folder he needed and passed it to his son.

"Maren already knows. She's part of the 'among other things' package," Jared told him. He tapped the folder he'd just been handed. "I'll get back to you on this."

"Good." Jared began to leave. Brian called after him. "And, Jared—"

Jared pivoted on his heel, turning to face his father again. "Yes?"

"This is just between us." He saw a hint of a skeptical look pass over Jared's face. "Lila doesn't want her kids knowing anything about this."

"But they're on the force," Jared protested. It seemed only logical that she would have said something to them first.

"Those are her wishes. Until she changes her mind, no one else finds out—least of all Zack, Taylor, Riley or Frank."

"Okay." He had no problems with following orders.

"But just so you know, 'kids' don't take kindly to their parents keeping things from them."

Brian laughed. Jared had no idea how protective parents could be, what lengths they were willing to go to in order to keep something harmful from reaching their children. "Just wait, your turn'll come."

Jared wasn't altogether sure if that was a theme and variation on "wait until you have children of your own" but the words stopped him dead. About to leave, he crossed back to his father's desk.

"How do you know that?"

He'd meant it as a general, throwaway line but the expression on Jared's face told him he'd managed to accidentally stumble onto something. What, he had no idea. So he did what he used to do with felons who wouldn't volunteer information. He bluffed.

"Did you really think you could keep it from me?" he asked incredulously. "I'm the chief of detectives, Jared, I know everything."

The thunder stolen from him, Jared set the folder back on the desk and crossed his arms before him. "Okay, smart guy, what's it going to be?" he challenged.

Stuck, Brian considered admitting his bluff, then decided to stretch it out a little more. He had nothing to lose. "You're going to have to be a little more specific in your question."

"Don't get cagey, old man. The baby," Jared enunciated. "What's it going to be?"

In the face of monumental news, the bluff was abandoned. "Baby?" Brian echoed in suppressed excitement. "What baby? Maren's pregnant?"

He'd been had, Jared thought. "Damn, you suckered me in, didn't you, old man?"

Brian laughed out loud, not at the expression on Jared's face but at the prospect of yet another Cavanaugh coming into the world.

"It's a father's job." He clapped his son on the back. "A baby." A broad grin split his face. "How soon?"

Jared thought of the expression on Maren's face as he left her this morning. "Not soon enough for Maren, she's sick to her stomach."

"Which is as flat as a board," Brian recalled. "I just saw her a week ago. Are you sure she'd going to have a baby?"

Because it meant so much to her, Maren had gone through five pregnancy tests—all with the same results—before she'd finally had the courage to go to her doctor. Jared nodded in answer to his father's question. "She's three months along and it's a secret."

Summer was coming. His daughter-in-law wasn't going to be able to hide behind layers of clothing. "Not for much longer."

He knew that, but for now, he was playing along. "I'm humoring her. She's the one throwing up, not me—as she reminds me most mornings."

Thrilled, Brian impulsively threw his arms around his son and hugged him. There was never a shortage of displays of emotion amid the Cavanaughs, especially when there was good news. "Welcome to the harried father's club."

"You were never a harried father," Jared told him once he was released.

A lot he knew, Brian thought. "I hid it well. When can I know? Officially, I mean," he added. He didn't know how long he could contain himself. Or keep from calling Andrew.

"I'll ask her," Jared promised, picking up the file again. "Meanwhile—" he nodded toward it "—I'll get on this."

Brian thought of Lila, of what she'd gone through and was still going through. He felt a little guilty over being so happy. "I appreciate that."

At the door, Jared began to pull it closed behind him. "See you, 'Grandpa,'" was his parting shot.

Brian had always thought he'd hate the sound of that when the name was finally applied to him. But he didn't. He liked it.

Liked it a lot. And he couldn't stop smiling for the rest of the day.

Lila frowned to herself. Brian was due over any minute and she still hadn't found it, much less gotten it out of the way. She *knew* she'd put the folder that contained all the unpaid bills right there on the small desk next to the kitchen counter. That's where it always was.

Except for now.

She was supposed to write out checks before Brian came by. Every week she'd toss the incoming bills into the folder and every Friday she'd sit down to sort through them and pay whatever was due.

But the folder was nowhere to be seen. She'd already spent the past thirty minutes looking, trying to recall the last time she'd seen it. There were so many things she did by rote that remembering was next to impossible at times.

She sighed, trying her best to work backward in her mind.

The folder wasn't the first thing that had developed legs of its own. A couple of days ago, the book she was currently reading had turned up in Riley's old room. When she'd asked Riley if she liked the book, Riley had no idea what she was talking about. And no recollection of even having touched the book, much less bringing it into her daughter's old room.

Lila was beginning to wonder if life was getting to her. The phone calls had stopped coming right after Brian had a tap put on her phone. But not the feeling of intrusion. Her favorite sweater disappeared right after that. And the glasses she'd washed and put away were back in the sink when she'd come home yesterday.

She was really starting to doubt herself.

Maybe she needed a change, to get away from everything for a while. Or permanently. She'd once had plans to sell this house and move into something smaller when the last of the children moved out. She remembered that Ben had been all for it. But that was just before he was shot and everything changed.

In all honesty, after everything that had happened, she couldn't see herself living anywhere else. Couldn't see herself giving up all the memories woven into the framework of every room. That was why she'd turned down the one offer she'd had.

Still, she didn't like the uneasiness, the feeling that there was something, a presence here, hovering about when she walked in at night. Having Brian around helped, but it didn't entirely dispel the feeling.

The doorbell rang and she flew to it, stopping only to glance through the peephole before she opened it.

"Hi," she murmured, stretching up on her toes to brush her lips against his.

Picking up where he'd left off years ago, Brian was immediately in tune with her. One look at her face told him something was wrong.

"What's the matter?" He wanted to know.

She shook her head. "Nothing, I just misplaced something." She walked back into the kitchen as she answered.

"Happens to me sometimes. It's not because you're getting old." He second-guessed what was running through her head. "You've got a lot on your mind." Taking her by the shoulders, he directed her to the table. "You sit down, I'll make you something for dinner."

She had to stop depending on him, letting him do things for her. "That's my job."

"Not tonight." Crossing to the refrigerator, he opened it to see what he had to work with. Andrew had rubbed off on him over the years and he'd gotten pretty good at whipping things up out of leftovers.

Staring inside, he paused for a second, then called to her over his shoulder. "Lila?"

"Yes?"

"Are bills easier to face when they're chilled?"

She had absolutely no idea what Brian was talking about. Rising from the table, she walked up behind him. "What?"

Turning, Brian held up a folder. *The* folder. The one she'd spent so much time looking for. "This was in the refrigerator," he volunteered. "Next to the milk."

Chapter 9

Lila stared at the folder Brian was holding as if it was some sort of a foreign object. "I didn't put it there," she protested, taking it from him.

How the hell had it gotten into the refrigerator?

"Maybe it hopped in by itself," Brian suggested whimsically. "Death by frostbite?"

"It's not funny, Brian," she insisted. "I don't know how it got there. Am I losing my mind?"

The look of distress in her eyes got to him. Brian searched for a way to comfort her. "Honey, we do so many things without thinking—"

At any other time, the term of endearment, used for the first time, would have been savored and cherished.

But right now, she was too upset to focus on anything but the cool folder she held in her hand.

"I don't put folders into the refrigerator," she said tersely, struggling not to lose her temper. Things were spinning out of control, beyond her reach and she didn't know how to fix it.

"Let me finish," he told her, his tone patient. "We do so much that sometimes we get things confused. Put a spoon in the medicine cabinet, a folder in the refrigerator. You've had a lot on your mind lately, one of which," he injected a sidebar, trying to get her to rise above her concerns, "I'd like to think is me—"

Lila cut him off, shaking her head. "I did *not* put the folder in the refrigerator. I haven't even opened the refrigerator since I came home and this damn folder was on the desk in the back room when I left for work this morning."

Brian looked at her for a long moment, trying to get her to center her thoughts. "You're sure?"

"Of course I'm sure. It's always there." The words rushed out of her mouth. If she said them fast enough, she could outdistance the doubts that crowded her mind. But she failed. "No, I'm not sure." Defeated, she sank down on a kitchen chair facing the refrigerator. She bumped the table with her hip. "I'm just so used to seeing it there, I just assumed…"

He nodded. "Could one of your kids have come in and accidentally—"

Her head jerked up. "And accidentally what? Put the

folder into the refrigerator? Why would they? They don't have anything to do with my bills and they don't come over unless I'm here. If they want to see me, they usually stop by the office at the precinct and we get caught up there." She looked accusingly at the folder she'd tossed on the kitchen table. "It just doesn't make any sense."

Moving behind her, Brian dropped his hands on her shoulders. Silently he let her know that he was here for her. That, like old times, he had her back no matter what.

"Don't waste time making too much of this," he advised. "These things happen."

Without thinking, she placed her hand over his, taking comfort from the contact. "They've been happening too often."

Brian dropped his hands and came around to face her. "Back up. What are you saying?"

She hadn't told him before. She supposed part of her kept hoping she was being absentminded. But now she thought someone was coming in while she was gone. But why? To what end? Things were moved around but nothing had been taken.

Lila regretted saying anything, but it was too late to take back the words. So she told him. "That things are out of place a lot lately."

Interest flared in his gray eyes but his expression remained the same. "Such as?"

"Such as the glasses that I made a special point of

washing and putting away before I left for work were back in the sink when I came home again." She watched his face, wondering if he thought she was going crazy. But if he was entertaining the thought, there was no indication on his face. "Such as the book that I had on my nightstand because I was reading a few pages every night turning up in Riley's room. Riley hadn't even been over that week," she added before he could ask. She frowned as she told him the latest occurrence prior to the wayward folder. "Such as my favorite sweater disappearing out of my closet and turning up in the pantry."

That sounded like an awful lot of coincidences, Brian thought, but it still might be possible. "There's usually a simple explanation for these things."

"Right." Frustrated, she blew out a breath as she ran her hand through her hair. "The early onset of dementia."

Brian's voice was serious as he said, "Discounting that for a second, *have* you asked your kids if they've inadvertently moved some of your things around?" Their days ran together, maybe she just hadn't noticed something was misplaced until she needed it—like the folder.

"I asked Riley about the book and Taylor if she borrowed my sweater." Lila paused, banking down the wave of anxiety that emerged out of nowhere. What if she was the one who was responsible for moving things around? Was it just a matter of stress, the way Brian suggested, or something more? She really didn't like going there. "I didn't say anything else because—"

"Yes, I know. You didn't want them worrying," he finished the sentence for her. It was getting a little old at this point. The younger McIntyres ranged from twenty-three to twenty-six and didn't need to be coddled. If he knew them, they'd be insulted by the mere suggestion that their mother thought they needed to be sheltered.

"No," Lila countered sharply, annoyed that he was second-guessing her, "because I didn't want them thinking their mother was losing her grip on reality."

He had another suggestion for her. "Could someone else be doing it?"

She'd been trying to understand why someone would break in and not take anything. That they would break in to play mind games was even more mystifying.

"You mean, gas-lighting me like in that old movie where the husband tries to make the wife think she's going crazy?" Brian nodded. "Who?" It was a logical question. She didn't know anyone who would want to do that to her.

"If we had the answer to that, we'd have the answer to 'why,' as well," Brian pointed out. Since she seemed to be of sound mind and she was sure none of her kids was playing musical possessions, then his theory held water. "For now, just assume that someone's been coming in while you're at work and moving things around. Maybe you should think about having a security system put in."

That was for people who owned things of value. She had nothing worth taking. Her most precious objects were only that because of sentimental value.

"I have a security system," Lila answered, nodding

at the dog lying across the kitchen threshold like a furry obstacle course.

Brian glanced at the sleeping dog. "Obviously it's not working." He didn't like the idea of her being here alone at night and he couldn't always come over. "Look, why don't you come and stay at my place for a while?" Anticipating her protest, he was quick to add, "Both of you."

"And have whoever's trying to pull this off think that they won? That they've succeeded in chasing me out of my own home?" She tossed her head indignantly. "Hell, no."

Brian shook his head, pushing a lock of hair from her face. "Not that I don't find your spirit incredibly sexy, but maybe for once you should listen to my advice."

He made it sound like she made a point of always going against him. "I listen to your advice," Lila countered.

Her memory seemed a bit faulty, he thought. "Right, when you agree with it."

Lila grinned, seeing no contradiction. "That's still listening."

He refused to be drawn into her smile, into her eyes. They had a serious problem on their hands.

"Like you said, this isn't funny. For whatever reason, someone's targeted you." He hated even saying it, much less believing it to be true. "Do you have any idea why?"

"Not a one." Lila feathered her fingertips along the furrow that had formed just above his eyes, gently smoothing it out. "Look, now that you found my folder and I can pay my bills, why don't we have that dinner you promised me?" Her smile turned wicked. "And then we can go on to dessert."

Removing her hand, he held it for a moment as he said, "Using sex to distract me doesn't change the problem, Lila."

She was on her toes, her lips lightly grazing the side of his neck. She felt a pulse jump just beneath them. "I know."

Brian felt her breath along his skin. Felt himself responding with such speed and intensity, he could have easily been in his adolescence again, instead of revisiting it. Damn but she did things to his head, scrambled his brain and made him one huge, pulsating mass of desire.

"I take it…you've decided…to skip…dinner."

"Dessert was always my favorite part," she breathed, winding her arms around his neck and raising her mouth up to his. Her body supple and pliant against his. His for the taking.

"Mine, too," he told her just before he pulled her to him and kissed her.

It only got better, Lila thought. Better and more intense. But how could you possibly improve on perfection, she wondered.

The first time they'd made love, it was exquisite, everything she'd ever dreamed of. And yet, it just kept getting better. Making love with him, the *anticipation* of making love with him, made her feel as if she could bend steel with her bare hands and leap tall buildings in a single bound.

Even in the midst of a dire situation, she clung to the promise of their next coming together, their next coupling. She lived for it.

She found that Brian didn't hurry even though he knew the path and even though he knew the exquisite ecstasy waiting for him at journey's end. He took his time, exploring every nuance all over again, as if he knew that no matter how many times he made love with her, there was always something new to discover, something new to experience.

For her the sameness never registered, because it wasn't the same. The thrill, the surprise, the wild explosions and ever-changing, mind-boggling profusion of colors, was there, waiting to engulf her.

If there was regret, it was because she'd allowed so much time to go by without making her feelings for him known. But then, until just recently, there'd been obstacles in the way. When they'd been together originally, he'd had a wife and four children and she'd had a husband and four children of her own.

Life, for her and for him, had been a tightrope walk. She knew that there was no telling what Ben would have done if she'd ever given in to her desire and made love with Brian. At the very least, Ben would have dragged her into court, loudly declared her an unfit mother and taken her children away from her. The "very most" had a finality about it that would have made her blood run cold if she spent any time thinking about it. Ben was not a man to be crossed.

But it was very hard to think right now, when her blood was so heated.

Brian took her on the kitchen table, pushing things aside and sending them flying down to the tiled floor. As she heard the napkin holder and the salt and pepper shakers clink and thump, despite the energy vibrating between them, she couldn't resist grinning at him. "Good thing nothing's made of glass."

His eyes pinned her in place. The desire she saw there almost made her stop breathing. "I'm good for it," he told her.

Exhilaration filled her, sharing space with anticipation. "Damn, but you are," she whispered.

She wore a navy-blue pencil skirt. He had it pushed up above her waist in less than a heartbeat, stripping her of her lace panties in the next moment. The palms of his hands replaced the feel of the whisper-soft material against her flesh. And then his fingers were there instead, slowly massaging her.

Lila arched, biting her lower lip to keep from crying out as the first volley exploded within her. She felt herself being pushed back until she was flat against the tabletop. And then came the feel of his lips, the flickering, teasing of his tongue as it took the explosion she'd experienced and turned it into a light show that filled every available space with stars and lightning bolts.

The thrust of his tongue effectively reduced the parameters of her world to the limited space of the rectangular table. And him.

"Now," she cried with a trace of desperation. "Now."

Lila had no more words to elaborate, but he knew what she was saying. What she wanted.

Exactly what he wanted.

The next moment he was inside her, hard and urgent. The climax that came shook them both down to their very core.

Lila clung to him long after her peak had leveled off. Clung to him until her breathing had returned to almost normal. The thumping of her heart against her rib cage, however, was going to take longer to dissipate and reach its regular rhythm.

She had never known it could be like this. Never known that the act of lovemaking could get better rather than slipping into a routine sameness.

Slowly, very slowly, air was replenished in her lungs. But the room still insisted on spinning around. "I may have the table bronzed."

She felt his mouth curve against hers, felt his smile before she saw it. "We'll add it to the collection," he told her.

She knew he was referring to the fact that aside from her bed, they were slowly making love on every flat and semiflat surface in the house, as well as against the wall beside the staircase in the hallway.

Lila smiled at him. She'd always known deep down that she loved him. But she'd never known the extent or that it was possible to love someone so much that her insides literally ached.

But saying so would scare him. Men didn't want to hear declarations of love. They were far more into the physical aspects of loving than the ethereal ones. After what he'd been through with Susan, her moods and her ultimate suicide, Lila doubted that Brian would ever truly be willing to leave himself open to love, or welcome it from her.

So she kept the words to herself. But even so, she felt as if she needed to say something to give him an inkling of what she was feeling.

She couched it in words as nonthreatening as she could find. "When we make love like this, nothing else matters. Everything else just fades away and I know that whatever's wrong will be okay."

He didn't quite feel that way. Even though she had him completely wrapped up around her little finger when they made love, once the euphoria faded, the problems he'd been tackling up to that point returned. As unsettling as ever.

But he didn't want to worry her any more than he sensed she already was. So for the sake of her peace of mind, he said, "Yeah, me, too," and for now allowed it to go at that.

Lila slid off the table, pulling her skirt back into place. She bent down and picked up her panties, scrunching them up into a ball inside her hand. "You're a lousy liar, Chief Cavanaugh."

"Yeah, I've been told that," he allowed philosophically. And then his eyes gleamed. "But never by a seminude woman before."

"I'm not seminude."

He took her panties from her and held them up. "I rest my case."

She grinned, as urges began to flood her again. For the second time she wove her arms around his neck, bringing her body up against his.

Provocatively, she moved her hips against him and saw desire flare in his eyes. "First time for everything."

His eyes twinkled and he rested his hands on the swell of her moving hips. "How about a second time?"

Lila ran the tip of her tongue along the outline of her lips. "You're on."

His eyes swept over her from bottom to top. Lila felt thunder crashing in her chest. "I was hoping this time that you would be."

Her laughter drifted up the stairs with them.

He couldn't stay. Jared was coming over to his house to discuss the assignment he'd given him and tell him what he and the others had or hadn't found. He wished now that he'd told Jared to see him during office hours instead. But the sooner this was resolved, the sooner Lila could go on with her life.

So reluctantly, a little more than an hour later, Brian took his leave of her. He didn't tell her that he'd asked his sons and niece for help. Instead he told her that there was work he had to catch up on, a promise he'd made to the mayor.

She surprised him by offering to come back to the precinct with him to help.

He turned her down. "This is 'chief' stuff," he lied, pulling on his slacks while she sat in the bed, bathed in the light from the lamp and nothing more. Stirring him even as he struggled to leave. "Something that involves my eyes only."

She tossed her hair over her shoulder. "You're beginning to sound like a spy."

"Sometimes I feel like one," he admitted.

There was a reason for that. A great many security measures that had been implemented since 9/11 had robbed the country of its innocence and sense of invulnerability. He felt guilty hiding behind that and lying to her, but he knew that Lila would balk if she knew that he'd brought someone else—even family—into the investigation. Especially since he hadn't told her anything about that investigation. As far as she knew, the only part he'd played was getting a trace put on her phone. And that seemed to have proven unnecessary since the calls had ceased.

Lila cocked her head. Her hair dipped sensuously over her breasts. "I can't convince you to stay?"

If she only knew the power she had over him. He cupped her cheek as he looked down into her face.

"Lila, you could convince me to shave my head and become a Tibetan monk—as long as my time up there involved you. But I'm hoping that isn't on your agenda."

"No, no monks. Only you." She caught his arm just as he began to draw away. "Will you come back tonight?"

He wanted to. God knew he wanted to, but he had a feeling this was going to take a while. He shook his head. "Probably not."

"I'll keep a light in the window anyway," she promised. Tugging on his arm to get him to bend over, she kissed him one more time, then scrambled out of bed. "Wait, I'll walk you down."

"No, stay," he told her. "I know my way out and I'd rather remember you just like that." His eyes swept over her and then he winked as he finally tore himself away.

It was only after she'd heard the front door close, the lock falling into place, that the phone beside her rang.

Picking the receiver up, she said, "Hello?"

There was nothing on the other end and she instantly thought it was her night caller. This was earlier than usual, but the way her hair stood up at the back of her neck, she knew she was right. It had to be him.

She was about to hang up when she thought she heard more than just a sound on the other end of the line. A single word.

As she jerked the receiver back up, she demanded, "What did you say?"

"Bitch."

The word resonated against her ear, as clear as a ringing church bell. Assaulting her and worse than that. It made her feel vulnerable again.

Chapter 10

Lila's hand trembled, and that bothered her to no end.

More than anything, she wanted to slam down the receiver, to break the connection that had brought this ghoul into her house, into her life. But that was exactly the reaction this man wanted: an outward demonstration of her fear. She was certain he would feed on her vulnerability. Slamming down the phone was just another way of displaying fear. Of symbolically running away.

So she held her ground and the receiver. "Why don't you stop playing these cowardly games and tell me who you are?" she demanded in a deadly calm voice. "Tell me what you hope to accomplish with all these soundless calls and playing musical possessions with my things, because I don't have time for guessing games. Unlike you, I have a life."

In response to her words, she heard a click on the other end of the line. And then the connection went dead. An iciness spread from her fingertips throughout her entire body.

This had to stop.

"Sorry, Dad," Jared apologized as he stood in the kitchen and accepted a bottle of beer from his father. "There are just the usual rumors, nothing more. I talked to Troy and Callie before coming here and they came up against the same dead end." Pausing to take a long swig, he recited exactly what he and the others had heard after several days of discrete inquiries. "Word has it that Ben McIntyre and his partner were executed by the same guy, a Jose Diaz who was part of the Del Rey Colombian drug cartel."

"Jose Diaz," Brian echoed. The name meant nothing to him.

Jared nodded. "Probably their version of John Doe," he theorized. "At any rate, as far as any of us could come up with, nobody else has been bragging that they offed two cops muscling in on the cartel's territory. Or even that there was one cop who paid for trying to rob the cartel."

After the bust had gone down—and the money went missing—what remained of the cartel seemed to have vanished. "Roberto Del Rey could have had this Jose Diaz do his dirty work for him, then taken back the money and gotten rid of Diaz."

Jared considered the scenario and saw no reason to challenge it. "As good a working theory as any, I guess," he said with a half shrug. He took another sip before adding, "Why are you asking, anyway? Something new come to light?"

Brian deliberately kept his answer vague. "No, I just told Lila McIntyre I'd look into it for her."

Jared cocked his head, studying his father's face. "She wants her late husband's name cleared?"

"She wants answers," Brian countered. He didn't like lying, especially not to his family, but he'd given Lila his word that he wouldn't go into detail. It wasn't that he didn't trust Jared to keep things secret. Jared had gone undercover more than once and knew how to keep a vast array of secrets from surfacing. He just didn't feel at liberty to break his word to Lila. At least, not without a damn good reason.

Jared nodded and seemed genuinely disappointed that he didn't have more information. "'Fraid she's going to have to do without those answers unless something fresh turns up."

"Tell your brother and cousin I appreciate the time they put in on this."

"Hey, what's family for?" He was about to say something else when the sound of a ringing cell phone scissored its way between them, cutting the conversation short. Both men automatically checked the devices clipped on their belts. Jared's was dormant. "Yours," he told his father, nodded at his father's cell phone.

Brian sighed. Now what? Slipping the phone out of its case, he flipped it open and crisply announced his name. "Cavanaugh."

"Brian, he just called."

He'd left Lila only a short while ago and he definitely hadn't expected to hear from her so soon. If her phone had rung so quickly after he left, was her house being watched or was it just a coincidence? Moreover, there was more than a little tension in her voice. "Something different about this call?" he asked. Out of the corner of his eye, he saw Jared put down his beer, becoming alert.

"He called me a bitch."

Anger flared through him so quickly it took him by surprise. He banked it down. "Did you recognize the voice?"

"Not from just one word." Lila paused, debating saying anything. More than likely, she was just being stupid for even thinking what she was thinking.

"But?" he prodded.

She might as well tell him and get it out. "But it sounded like…Ben."

She was overwrought, Brian thought. He should have never left her tonight. "Ben's dead," he reminded her.

"I know, I know," she said, her tone worn and restless

at the same time. "I saw the body." She sighed again, trying to get hold of herself. Of course it hadn't been Ben. How could it? "It's just the strain and maybe some residual guilt."

The last word caught his attention. "Meaning?"

Damn, she was unraveling, Lila thought. If she wasn't careful, she was going to drive Brian away. But she was nothing if not honest and she couldn't stop now. "I can't help it. You're the first man I've been with since Ben's murder. The only other man I've ever been with except for Ben." There, he might as well know everything. "A part of me feels like I'm cheating on my vows." In this day and age, he probably thought she was some kind of a throwback. "It's crazy, I know."

But rather than agree with her assessment, he quietly said, "Me, too."

Relief flooded through her like welcomed rain after a summer draught. Her knees almost gave way. "Oh, God, you don't know how much better that makes me feel."

Brian could feel Jared's eyes on him. This wasn't the time to go into any personal details with Lila. "I'll be right over," he promised her.

She didn't want to drag him back, didn't want to come across like some helpless damsel in distress. That wasn't the image she had of herself.

But even so, her protest was only halfhearted. "You don't have to—"

"Yes, I do," he told her firmly. "Don't open the door until I get there."

The last instruction was entirely unnecessary. "I am a cop, Brian."

"I know, that's why I'm worried." He knew what she was capable of. God forbid her caller was hanging around and tried to get in. "You're fearless—but not invulnerable. Hang in there."

After closing his cell phone, he slipped it back into his case. Jared still stood there, patiently eyeing him and waiting.

"Anything you want me to do?" he asked the moment the connection was broken.

Right now, the only instructions he had were for the man who had installed the tap on Lila's phone. "Go back to your pregnant wife before she has my head for giving you an off-duty assignment."

But Jared made no move to leave. "If you need anything—"

Brian nodded. He appreciated the offer. "I know who to call. Really, Jared, until I can run this down, there isn't anything for you to do."

He was his father's son and despite efforts to the contrary, his curiosity had been aroused. "That was Lila, wasn't it?" Jared prodded. "Has this got something to do with Ben's death?" Following that line of thinking, he took a further stab at it. "Someone think she has the money that disappeared?"

God, he hoped not, Brian thought as he walked out of the house. Jared followed in his wake. "I don't know. But, yes, that was Lila. That's all I can tell you for now.

And even that you have to keep to yourself," he cautioned.

"You haven't told me anything yet," Jared pointed out. Brian deactivated the alarm system on his vehicle. "That's not exactly a hard secret to keep."

Brian opened the door on the passenger side. "Give Maren my love."

"I gave her mine," Jared quipped. "I think that's what got me into the doghouse in the first place." And then he grinned broadly from ear to ear. "Still can't get used to thinking I'm going to be a father."

"It'll hit you like a ton of bricks that first night," Brian promised. "Right after you bring the baby home from the hospital."

Jared put his hand on his father's arm just before Brian slipped into the car. Brian eyed him quizzically. "Call me if you need anything—on or off the record."

"You'll be the first," Brian told him just before he shut his door.

He got to Lila's house in record time. Knocking, he called out her name, announcing himself. When she opened the door, he saw that she'd abandoned her robe and had gotten dressed again.

"Are you all right?" Even as he asked, his eyes swept over her. He wanted to ascertain her condition for himself.

The smile she offered was small and sad, as if she were disappointed in herself. "I'm fine. I feel a little like a wimp, calling you like that."

"You did the right thing."

Closing the door behind him and then locking it, Brian took her into his arms and kissed the top of her head. It amazed him how easily this had evolved, how comfortable he was, holding her. How well she fit into his arms.

"And for the record, you feel like a sexy woman, not a wimp." Releasing her, he crossed over to the telephone in the living room. "I contacted Manny Lopez on my way over here." To make ends meet, the man occasionally pulled double duty. Lopez was still at the lab when he'd called. It made things easier. "He was able to get the number of the caller." He heard the small intake of breath even though he knew she was trying to stifle it. "The call was made on one of those disposable phones."

She made no effort to hide her disappointment. "So we don't know where the call came from."

"No, but we can still trace the phone's serial number through the server and find out where the phone was bought." It was a good news, bad news type of situation. "I doubt it was bought with a credit card. Whoever purchased it probably paid cash, but if we're lucky," he ended on an up note, "the store'll have a surveillance camera."

"If we're lucky," she echoed. A lot of stores just put up fake cameras, unwilling to bear the expense of a real surveillance system.

"Personally—" reaching out, he gently touched her face "—I feel very lucky."

She laughed softly. If nothing else, this awful ordeal

had brought Brian and her back into each others' lives with astonishing results.

"Yeah, me, too." She paused for a second, then decided she had nothing to lose by asking. "Did you mean what you said earlier?" He looked a tad confused, so she elaborated. "About feeling guilty?"

He hadn't wanted to dwell on that or to make her feel that making love with her caused him to think of Susan. But they couldn't get away from the fact that he had residual feelings to work out of his system. But he intended to do it alone.

"Not anything that I wanted to burden you with," he told her.

Didn't he know by now that he could tell her anything? That she wanted to know what bothered him?

"It doesn't. It makes me feel that maybe I'm not being a basket case. It has nothing to do with love," she qualified, afraid that he might think she still had feelings for Ben and that was why she felt guilty. "I stopped loving Ben a long time ago." She raised her eyes to his and the words just came out. "About the time I started loving you." Lila sighed. "Damn."

"Damn?"

"I wasn't supposed to say that." She dragged her hand through her hair, impatient with herself. "Look, I don't want you to think that I'm trying to make you feel that I expect something from you. I—"

He smiled at Lila. "You definitely talk too much sometimes."

"Yes, I know."

Taking her face in his hands, he kissed her long and hard. Because, even though he couldn't say it out loud, because there was a whole spectrum of fear attached to it, he knew he loved her. But loving someone wasn't as easy as he'd once believed.

After the kiss ended, he held Lila and gave her as much comfort as he could. He found he received the same for himself. Holding her made him feel better.

"It's going to be all right, Lila," he promised quietly, whispering the words into her hair. "We'll find whoever's doing this."

We, she thought. Not quite. "In case you haven't noticed, I'm not exactly taking an active participation in all this," she pointed out. "Other than picking up the phone and noticing that things have been misplaced."

He knew that had to frustrate her. It would him. "If we have any leads at all, I promise I'll let you know."

"You keep saying 'we.' Who's 'we'?" Lila stepped back to look at his face. "Did you bring anyone else into this?" The moment she asked, she had her answer. Because they'd spent so much time in one another's company all those years they were partnered, she could read him like the proverbial book. "You did." She sighed, trying not to get upset. She trusted Brian. He wouldn't break his word unless it was with good reason. "Who?"

Cornered, he had to admit it. He could no more lie outright to her than he could to anyone in his family. "Jared, Troy and Callie."

She closed her eyes. "Oh, God." The next moment her eyes flew opened again. "Do they know about the phone calls?"

"All I said was that I wanted to find out if anyone ever took any credit for killing Ben and his partner, Walker. Whoever killed them either has the money or is looking for the money," he theorized. Though he hated himself for it, he was too much of a cop not to watch her face for a reaction, a slight sign that could implicate her with the missing money. But there was no change in her expression. "That's all any of them know," he swore, then was forced to add, "but I didn't raise any dummies."

"No," Lila agreed, "but you Cavanaughs are an honorable bunch." Just like her own children, she thought. "Even if they make the connection, we can keep this contained. And if we wind up needing extra help, luckily there's almost an army of you." Her smile was self-deprecating as she made her apology. "I didn't mean to make you come back."

He should have never left, he upbraided himself again. "That's all right, I was finished anyway and there's no place else I'd rather be." He nodded toward the stairs. "Why don't you go up to bed? I'm going to stay up for a while."

"So am I," she informed him. She was way past the point when someone could tell her when to go to bed. "I'll go get the cards," she volunteered.

That struck a familiar note. Back in the day, they used to play poker by the hour when they were on a stakeout.

"Want some coffee?" she asked before she left the room.

There were times when he thought he lived on coffee. He could give anything else up but that. "Sounds good to me."

Lila stopped just before she crossed the threshold into the kitchen and glanced at him over her shoulder. "Brian?"

"Yes?"

"I really appreciate you going out of your way like this."

He brushed off her thanks. "It's not out of my way. Besides, what are friends for?"

She nodded, forcing a smile to her lips. "What, indeed?"

Friends, Lila thought, walking into the kitchen. He'd referred to himself as her friend. After she'd slipped and admitted she loved him. It told her what she'd already assumed. That when it came to this relationship, they were in different places. But then, it wasn't anything more—or less—than she'd expected.

But far less than she secretly wanted.

"We got lucky," Troy told his father a couple of days later. He and Callie met with Brian in the computer tech lab. His cousin motioned for the computer technician to move aside for a minute. When he did, she took over the keyboard. "Lopez managed to use the serial number to trace it back to the store where the cell phone was originally purchased. J & B Electronics. Oakland," he elaborated. "The owner wasn't really keen on parting with the surveillance tapes, but Callie—" he nodded toward his cousin with a pleased grin "—persuaded him."

"He had a lot of outstanding parking tickets," she said, her fingers flying across the keyboard as if they were independent entities. Glancing over her shoulder at her uncle, she flashed a wide grin. "We made a trade. The tapes for the tickets. If you notice—" she indicated the computer monitor "—lucky for us, they're all time and date stamped. Most of the tapes were incredibly boring, but we did get our man—or our couple."

"Couple?" Brian echoed. He moved to stand directly behind Callie. The room was fairly dark, making the action on the screen a little clearer, but it was still somewhat fuzzy.

"A man and a woman," Callie told him just as the couple came into camera range. "They look like they're arguing before they come up to the register. The woman seems far from happy."

"Probably means they're married," the computer tech guessed. "Married people always argue." He became aware that both of the younger Cavanaughs had turned to look at him. He raised his hands as if to wave away his words. "Present company excepted, of course."

"Of course," Troy repeated, suppressing his amusement.

Brian hardly heard the exchange. The couple had

drawn closer to the register and the camera. The hairs on the back of his neck rose as if the air had suddenly gone bone-dry.

"Hold it," he ordered Callie. "Can you freeze that shot?"

"Freeze it, thaw it, I can make it do tricks if you want," Callie quipped.

"Just enlarge it," Brian told her, his voice deadly serious.

"The couple?" she asked before she struck the keys.

His eyes didn't move from the screen. "No, just the man."

"Your wish is my command," Callie replied.

Brian stared at the enlarged shot. It was incredibly grainy. "Can you clean it up a little more?"

"I'll do what I can, but those forensic shows on TV get it wrong. There's only so much you can do with software." She hit a few more keys with minimal effect. "That's as good as it gets," she apologized.

It wasn't quite enough to be absolutely conclusive for him, but still caused a chill to slither down his spine.

As Brian examined the fuzzy photo, he could swear that the man buying the disposable cell phone looked a hell of a lot like Ben McIntyre.

Chapter 11

Brian grew very quiet. He felt rather than saw Troy turn to look at him.

"What's the matter, Dad?" Troy asked. "You look as if you've seen a ghost."

"Ghosts don't buy cell phones," Brian murmured, still looking at the image in disbelief. Was it possible? Or just the power of suggestion? Was Ben McIntyre actually still alive?

Then who was buried in McIntyre's grave?

Callie rose, surrendering the keyboard and computer back to the lab technician. The latter gladly reclaimed his seat.

Brian was already leaving the room. She hurried to

catch up to him. Both of her cousins were half a step behind her.

The second they were out of the lab, she asked, "Uncle Brian, is that Ben McIntyre?"

Brian stopped right outside the door. The tech had gone back to what he'd been doing previously and there was no one else in the hall but his sons and niece.

He looked at Callie closely, surprised by her question. "You knew Ben McIntyre?"

She nodded. "I worked with him once on a special detail. It was just when I was starting out. He seemed like an okay guy," she tagged on.

He was, Brian thought. Once.

Troy looked confused. "But isn't he's supposed to be dead?"

"Yes." Brian sighed. This was getting worse and worse. "He is."

Callie exchanged glances with Jared. "Could McIntyre have faked his own death for some reason?" Callie asked.

That's the way it was beginning to look, Brian thought. "Right now, anything is possible. Not a word of this gets around until I've had time to break the news—possible news to his widow."

"If McIntyre's alive, then she's not his widow," Jared commented.

"I know." Brian set his jaw grimly. And therein, he added silently, lay the problem.

* * *

He had a meeting scheduled first thing after lunch with the police chief. His first order of business was to have the meeting pushed back. He needed to talk to Lila first.

The chief, Jack Larsen, was a decent sort. Not as good at his job as Andrew had been before him, but he was sincerely trying. Personally taking Brian's call, the man then told him that his assistant would be in touch with a new time and date since the rest of his day was booked solid.

As he searched for words that would soften the blow for Lila, Brian barely heard what Larsen was saying to him. He took his cue from the silence on the other end of the line and made a polite reply, although for the life of him, he wasn't sure what it was he said. His mind, his focus, was elsewhere.

But Larsen sounded satisfied, so all was well.

Brian took the stairs rather than the elevator down to the second floor where Lila was currently working in the records department. Each step he took eerily clattered on the metal stairs like a death knell.

The office where she worked was all the way down the hall. When he reached it, Brian paused for a moment, watching her. Lila seemed utterly unaware that her whole world was about to be thrown on its ear.

And he was the one who was about to do it.

Responsibility weighed heavily on his shoulders. Lila had already been through so much, he really didn't want to be the one to destroy whatever peace she'd finally found.

But then, he knew he had to be the one to tell her about Ben. Because he cared about her.

And now, he thought cynically, she would remember that he was the one who'd set a match to her carefully restructured world.

Lila felt someone looking at her. Felt it as surely as if she'd been physically touched. Ever since this thing with the night caller had started, she'd been on her guard. It was paranoia for the most part, but still, she couldn't shake the feeling.

Better safe than sorry.

Glancing up, she saw Brian standing several feet from her desk. Instantly she smiled. But the warmth that filled her faded the next moment. Something in Brian's eyes set off an alarm in her. But why? He was the one she felt most comfortable with, the one who knew her thoughts, her secrets. Brian had her back, the way he'd always had.

"Brian? What's wrong?" Lila came around her desk to get closer to him. She lowered her voice. "You look as if you lost your best friend."

That would be you, he thought. Out loud, he said, "I hope to God not."

He'd called her his best friend more than once, so she knew he was referring to her.

"Okay, now you're scaring me." And then, because it was the nature of the job, her heart suddenly froze in her chest. "Is it one of the kids? Did something happen to one of them? Is it Riley?" Riley was her most reck-less child, a daredevil ever since she first opened her eyes. "Or Zack?" Her mind was going a mile a minute as scenario after scenario occurred to her. "Taylor?" Oh, not her baby. "Not Frank." Her voice was almost hoarse.

Brian quickly shook his head as the names flew from her lips. "No, nothing's happened to any of them. They're all okay."

Lila felt almost dizzy with relief. On the heels of that came confusion. "Then what?" she prodded. "Why do you look like you have something to tell me that you really don't want to say?"

The laugh that emerged was short. She always could read him. "You have no idea how much I don't want to say this."

"Not comforting, Brian," she told him. Taking a deep breath, Lila nodded over to an area where the person-nel on the floor took their breaks. It was empty now. They could talk freely.

She led the way and Brian followed. Turning to him, she searched his face for clues and found none. "Is this official or unofficial?"

"Both."

Her uneasiness increased tenfold. "Bigger than a bread box?" Whenever she was nervous, she sought refuge in humor, thin though it was. She was aware that her knees didn't feel quite solid. But since whatever he had come to tell her didn't involve any of her children, she felt a little better about facing what he had to say.

Or so she thought.

"It's Ben."

The two words hung in the air like a bomb set to go off. Her stomach tightened and she felt the color drain from her face.

"What's Ben?" she asked, her voice hoarse with suppressed emotion.

God but he wished there was some way to keep this from her. "There's a chance he might still be alive."

It was a joke, a bad joke. Why was Brian being so cruel?

"That's impossible," she cried even though she realized that she'd been the one who'd said the caller's voice reminded her of Ben. Lila's blood ran cold in her veins. "I saw his body."

"You saw *a* body," he corrected. When she continued staring at him, he went on. "What you saw was the body of a man approximately the same height, the same coloring as Ben, wearing Ben's clothes, Ben's wedding ring. His fingerprints," he reminded her, "were gone—"

Desperate to negate what Brian was saying, she cut in. "That's because he was in the water for almost a week. The fish ate his fingers." They'd eaten away other parts of Ben, as well, and for the rest of her life, she was going to carry that image in her mind, no matter how hard she tried to block it out. While she'd forbidden any of her children to view the body, she had been the one to identify him—and spent the next few hours after she did throwing up in the ladies' room.

Brian hated having to bring up these details. At the time, because of where the body had washed up—in the same vicinity where his partner was found—and the clothes that the dead man was wearing, there hadn't been a question of who the body was.

But now, it was different. "Remember, his teeth were smashed in."

Tears shined her eyes, tears for the man she had once loved, tears for the man Ben had once been, before he began to change into someone she barely knew. Someone she no longer loved.

She glanced at Brian defiantly. "That's because we thought Ben had been tortured by whoever eventually killed him and Dean." Whether it was just payback or because the killer had tried to get information out of Ben, she didn't know, but the body had been horribly mutilated.

"I know. That was why we never did a DNA test. It seemed like a closed case." Now it seemed like a huge oversight. "Maybe we dropped the ball," he told her quietly.

She watched him for a long moment, pulling herself together. She had to stop feeling like a wife and start thinking like a police officer. "What makes you think that Ben is still alive?"

"We found a surveillance tape of the man buying the cell phone used to call you."

So it had been Ben calling. Why? Why didn't he just show himself? If he was alive, why hadn't he shown himself before now? Rose, Andrew's wife, disappeared for eleven years because she'd had traumatic amnesia. Was that what happened to Ben?

Somehow, she doubted it was that simple. Nothing was ever simple when it came to Ben. She raised her chin. "I want to see the tape."

Brian shook his head. "Lila, I don't think that's wise."

Lila dug in. "I'm not going for 'wise,' I'm going for rights. I'm not some fragile doll, don't treat me like one. If that's Ben on the tape, I have a right to see it," she told him. She realized that she'd allowed her temper to flare and it wasn't fair to Brian. She knew he was just trying to protect her. "Brian, please. All this time, I've been carrying around that awful image in my head of Ben's half-eaten body. I need a way to get rid of it. If Ben is still alive, I want to see proof."

There was no point in arguing with her, Brian thought. In her place, he'd say the same thing. "All right, come with me."

"Give me a minute." Going back into the office, she told the first person she saw, a temporary file girl, that the chief of detectives required her presence in the tech lab. The girl, fresh out of high school, began asking questions, but Lila was already walking back across the threshold.

"Okay," she told Brian, bracing herself for the ordeal ahead, "let's go."

* * *

Lila watched the image on the computer monitor in stony silence. Everything inside of her shut down. This couldn't be happening.

And yet, it was.

When the tech reran the sequence a second time, Lila nodded slowly. "That's him," she said, her voice barely a whisper.

"The quality of the tape is poor and grainy," Brian pointed out.

He could give all the excuses he wanted. She knew what she knew. "That's him."

He wanted to put his arms around her, to hold her and tell her it was going to be all right. But they were at work. The last thing she needed was another rumor circulating about her.

So instead he asked, "How can you be so sure?"

The second time around, she'd watched the way the man in the tape walked. That was when she knew for certain. "He broke his left ankle on our honeymoon. It never healed quite right and he tended to favor it just a little, especially when he was tired." She paused before adding in a grim voice, "Just like the guy in the surveillance tape."

Manny Lopez turned in his chair and looked at him. "Is this still under wraps?"

"I'll let you know when it's otherwise," Brian ordered.

Taking Lila by the arm, he escorted her out of the room. "You know what we have to do next." It wasn't really a question but a grim statement. There was only one thing *to* do.

Lila stared straight ahead of her and nodded. "I know."

"I need your permission."

She raised her eyes to his. "Do you think I'd say no?"

He'd been too concerned about her to entertain that idea. "Right now, I can't begin to imagine what you're going through."

The slightest hint of a smile curved her lips, fading in the next heartbeat.

"That makes two of us," she said ironically. "I'm too numb to really feel anything." She ran her tongue along lips that had gotten so dry she could almost feel the words brushing against them as they left her mouth. "Dig him up," she told Brian. "Or whoever we wound up burying instead."

She suddenly felt completely drained. And cold. She ran her hands up and down her arms, thinking she would ever rid herself of the chill that had descended over her.

When she finally spoke again, her words mingled with a sigh. "I guess, then, that was him I heard on the phone."

"Don't go getting ahead of yourself," Brian warned. He wanted her to cling to a positive outlook for as long as humanly possible. If he could have accomplished this without telling her, he would have, even though she would have been angry with him for withholding information. But there was no way around her knowing. "Let's dig up the body first."

"You know what we're going to find," she countered. And then it felt as if a ton of bricks had hit her. She covered her face with her hands, struggling for strength, for control. "Oh God, how could I have been so stupid? Why didn't I ask for a DNA test when he washed up on the shore?"

"For the same reason none of us thought of it at the time," he reminded her gently. "Everything pointed to it being Ben."

Lila blew out a long breath, doing her best not to come unglued. "I guess that was what Ben was counting on."

But if the man they'd buried wasn't Ben, why had he gone into hiding? Was he as guilty as everyone said? And who was the dead man? Had Ben killed him? Had he killed his partner, too?

How could you have done this to the kids? she demanded silently.

Weary, she glanced at Brian. "Do what you have to do." And even as she said it, her eyes widened as she realized something.

For the second time the blood seemed to drain out of her face. Brian took hold of her shoulders, afraid she was going to faint. "What?"

"This means I'm still married to him." Each word felt like a shard of glass. And then more thoughts assaulted her. "Oh God, we made love. What if he knows? What if he's been watching the house?"

He was going to put a surveillance detail together to watch the house, but he kept that to himself for the time being. "Lila, until we have the DNA results—and you know that's going to take time—I want you to put this out of your head."

"How?" she asked. This wasn't happening, she thought. It couldn't be. "Short of falling into a coma, how am I supposed to just 'forget' about this?"

"By being the strong woman you are," Brian told her simply. He could see a retort rising to her lips. He cut her short. "And by doing it for your kids."

"The kids," she echoed.

They deserved to know, and yet she didn't want to put them through this. Not until they were absolutely, positively sure. Right now, she just wanted it to all go away. But the nightmare had come back for her and it was real. Ben was alive. She didn't need a DNA test to tell her that. Her gut told her.

"I don't want them to know. Not yet. Not until the evidence is conclusive." Because maybe, just maybe, she was wrong and Ben was actually dead.

"They won't hear it from me," Brian promised solemnly.

She trusted him, but he wasn't the only one involved. "What about—?"

"Troy, Jared and Callie know enough not to say anything," he assured her. "And Manny knows his job's on the line if he tells anyone anything that goes on in the lab." She didn't look convinced. "Don't worry."

Brian took her hands in his. "I can have the body exhumed at night. Since you agree, the request doesn't have to go through the court. And if I rent the equipment myself, I don't even have to inform the higher authorities. This can be viewed as a private exhumation. We don't have to bring anyone into this beyond the people already involved."

But once the body was exhumed, the test still had to be run. Which meant that someone had to take a sample from the body. "What about the M.E.?" she asked. "He's going to have to take a sample—" But Brian was shaking his head. "He doesn't have to take a sample?"

"Patience can take a sample so that we can run the DNA test."

Patience. That was another niece, she recalled. The daughter of his dead brother, Mike. There was only one thing wrong with that. "Patience is a veterinarian."

"Patience has medical training," he told her, "and it doesn't take much to take a sample."

This was beginning to sound almost doable. "So no one needs to find out?"

That wasn't strictly true. "Not until we're sure," he qualified. "After that—"

She nodded. "I know, it becomes public." She thought of her sons and her daughters. And cursed Ben for putting them through this. "And then the shame starts all over again."

He knew she wasn't thinking of herself. Her mind was on her children, as his would be if he faced something like this. It was one of the many things that made him feel close to her.

"We're an advanced society, Lila," he told her. "The sins of the father are no longer visited on the sons and daughters. All four of them are damn fine cops. We'll all get through this," he promised. "Together. In the meantime, all of you are attending that party that I mentioned Andrew is throwing."

A party was the last thing she wanted to face. "I can't—"

"Yes," Brian said firmly, taking her hand and threading his fingers through hers, "you can. Don't make me pull rank on you."

A detective from the homicide division passed them and grinned broadly as he looked from one to the other. "Morning, Chief."

Brian nodded. So much for a low profile when it came to his private life. This was going to make the rounds before the end of the day. "Morning, Dempsey."

"And let the rumors begin," Lila murmured under her breath.

"I've never been afraid of rumors," he told her. "I didn't think that you were."

He knew how to get to her, she thought even as she felt herself reacting predictably. Knew just how to press her buttons.

"I'm not," she replied with feeling.

Brian nodded. "Good to hear." He continued to hold her hand as they walked to the elevator.

Chapter 12

"Heard you were seen holding hands with the chief of d's."

Startled, Lila turned from her desk to see Riley standing behind her, a whimsical smile playing across her younger daughter's face.

It was the next morning and they were both in early. As was her custom—when she wasn't completely swamped and behind in typing up her reports—Riley had stopped by her mother's office before officially going on duty. She tried to do it at least once or twice a week.

"Any truth in that?" Eyes the color of bright shamrocks pinned her as her daughter leaned a hip against her desk and waited for an answer.

Lila rolled her eyes, wondering what other rumors were spontaneously combusting throughout the building. "Oh God, I thought it would take a little longer to make the precinct rounds than just eighteen hours."

Riley had her answer. "So—" she pretended to study the brim of the hat she held in her hands "—it's true. You were holding hands with Brian Cavanaugh."

Had Zack said anything to his sister? Lila wondered, then dismissed the thought. Zack was as close-mouthed as a tomb. This was probably something passed on by word of mouth. She should have said something to the rest of her family about getting together with Brian rather than have them find out from outsiders.

"Riley, I—"

But her daughter held up her hand to stop whatever words were about to emerge in protest or explanation. "Mom, Mom, it's okay." She flashed a brilliant smile. "We like him."

"We?"

Riley twirled the hat before setting it rakishly on her head, looking more like the front woman for a band than a serious policewoman. "Zack, Taylor, Frank and me—"

"And I," Lila corrected automatically before she could stop herself.

"That's a given."

When Lila sighed, Riley added, "As a matter of fact, when I was a kid and things got kind of bumpy between you and Dad—" which was her polite way of saying that her father's yelling became almost intolerable "—I used to pretend that Brian Cavanaugh was my father." Riley smiled wistfully. "He was always so cool, so even-tempered. And he talked to me whenever he stopped by." Shrugging, she looked off through the window. The sky was a stunning shade of blue and the day promised to be beautiful. "Dad never seemed to have time for any of us."

Because she'd spent so much time trying to be the peacemaker, the one who kept things on an even keel at home, it was second nature to her to try to defend Ben's actions to one of her children. "Your father had a lot to deal with."

"So did you," Riley pointed out, "so did your partner. And Brian had four kids, just like Dad." She seemed to know the topic only raised bad memories. Very smoothly, Riley switched gears. "Anyway, that's all in the past." Leaning forward, she took her mother's hands in hers. "Dad's gone and you're not. You should have a shot at finding some happiness."

As gently as she could, Lila withdrew her hands. Inside she felt a fresh wave of guilt. Guilt because she still kept her loved one in the dark both about Ben possibly being alive and about her seeing Brian. "You're making too much of this."

Riley wasn't fooled. "I've got a hunch that maybe you're making too little of it. You shouldn't tell yourself lies and—" She fixed her mother with a look, doing her best to keep a straight face. "You shouldn't lie to your kids."

Lila's head jerked up as if she'd been pricked by a sharp needle.

"Mom, I'm only kidding." And then Riley peered more closely at her mother's expression. "Mom," she lowered her voice even though only one other person was in the vicinity, sitting all the way across the room, "is something wrong?"

Lila had always been a truthful person. Which was why she would have never betrayed her marriage vows and given in to her desire to sleep with Brian when they were partnered. Had she done that, she couldn't have kept it from her husband. Keeping this secret—that Ben might be alive—from her children was tantamount to lying in her eyes.

A sick gut feeling grew since Brian had asked her to exhume Ben's body. Lila knew Ben was alive. The truth would come out. It was just a matter of time. While she really didn't want to burden her children with all this— especially if it turned out *not* to be true—she didn't want them to be caught unaware.

Lila pressed her lips together, then made up her mind. The way she saw it, she had no choice. Rising, she motioned for Riley to follow her outside into the hall.

Once out of the office, Lila made sure they were alone. Three policemen approached. One she didn't recognize nodded his head at Riley while the other two tendered greetings as they passed. Lila waited until all three had turned the corner and disappeared from view.

"I've got something to tell you," Lila said, wishing there was a way to stretch out each word and that this was already out in the open and over with. Being a mother, she was never going to get over wanting to shield her children.

"I think I know what it is," Riley told her mother.

Lila was stunned. "You do?" This was supposed to be kept secret. Brian had promised her the news wouldn't leak out. "How?"

Riley's smile was amused. "Not too hard to figure out, really. Mom, you're an adult, it's okay."

All right, maybe Riley didn't know. This wasn't adding up. "What's okay?"

Riley brought her head down, her words hardly above a whisper. "Sleeping with the chief. Like I said, you deserve some happiness. And if he—"

Oh God, Lila wished it was all this simple, that admitting to being with Brian was the bombshell about to be dropped instead of the one she still harbored. "That's not what I wanted to tell you."

"But you are sleeping with him, right?"

Riley's eyes danced. "This isn't a proper conversation for a mother and daughter to be having," Lila protested.

"If the tables were turned, it would be," she reminded her mother.

Those days were long gone, Lila thought. These days Riley had more boyfriends than fingers. "You're twenty-four, Riley. At this point, a little bit of ignorance on my part might be a good thing."

"Okay, what did you want to talk to me about?"

"It's not that I want to," Lila told her ruefully. "I have to."

"Okay." She watched her mother's face closely.

"Riley, we think your father is alive."

The natural exuberance that had been part of Riley since the day she was born slipped away right before her eyes.

"Go on," Riley said quietly.

Lila steeled herself. As succinctly as possible, she told her daughter everything she hadn't wanted any of her children to be exposed to, omitting nothing, including the exhumation scheduled later that night.

Riley listened intently, making no comment until the end. "Then who's in Dad's grave?"

Lila shook her head. It was a question she'd asked herself over and over again since yesterday. "If it's not your father, then I haven't any idea."

Riley's eyes widened. "The drug cartel guy."

"What?"

"It makes sense," Riley insisted eagerly. "Everyone thought that Dad and his partner were killed by the guy they'd tricked into bringing them into the deal. Maybe the guy found out who they were and shot Walker. Then Dad shot him in self-defense."

They both knew that was only one scenario. A more likely one would be that Ben had killed the go-between not in self-defense but because he was in the way. After that, he'd made off with the money. Otherwise, why hadn't he come forward in all this time? Why had he let his family think he was dead?

But she knew how hard it had to be for Riley to think of her father being on the other side of the law, so she didn't try to offer an alternate theory.

"Maybe," Lila said.

Riley shoved her hands into her pockets. "You know, you should have told me about those calls when they started coming in."

"I didn't want you—any of you—" Lila emphasized, "to worry."

Riley laughed, her features softening. "Mom, we're cops, we're supposed to worry. It's part of the job description, remember? And so is protect and serve."

That worked both ways, Lila thought. "In case the fact temporarily slipped your mind, Riley, I'm a cop, too."

* "Yeah, but you're a mom," Riley teased, putting her arm around her mother's shoulders for a moment. "The rules are different." And then, out of the blue, she made an announcement. "I'm moving back in."

Lila's eyes met hers. "You are staying put," she said, mimicking Riley's tone. "You're entitled to a life of your own, Riley," she added firmly. "I've got things covered."

"The chief staying with you?"

Lila smiled, shaking her head. She wasn't about to step into that trap. If she admitted to a relationship with Brian, she knew her family. There would be expectations. And those very expectations might signal the death of whatever might be in their future, killing it before it ever had a chance to flourish. "You ask too many questions."

"I'll take that as a yes. Because if he's not staying with you, I'm moving back in."

Lila glanced at her watch. They could finish arguing about this later. "Get upstairs or you're going to be late for roll call."

Riley began to head down the hall to the elevators. "This isn't over yet," she promised, tossing the words over her shoulder.

"No," Lila agreed, not about to be browbeaten by someone she'd given birth to no matter how much she loved her. "Not while there's breath left in my body."

"You don't have to be here, you know."

There was a full moon out. Somehow, it seemed almost ghoulishly appropriate, given that she was standing in a cemetery. She'd stood in silence beside Brian as the large power shovel Jared was operating broke ground, biting into the earth and then spitting out the dirt to one side.

Every bite brought it closer to the casket buried below.

Closer to the truth.

She looked at Brian and smiled. When was he going to learn? "Yes, I do have to be here. I never did 'sitting on the sidelines' well, remember?" She sighed, her mind momentarily taking her elsewhere. "This damn desk job I have is killing me, Brian." She made a decision then and there. Life moved too fast for her to hang back and stand still. "I'm fully healed." She could see her statement had caught his attention. "I'm going to put in to get my old job back."

Surprised, Brian was silent for a moment. Only the noise of the machine filtered through the night air. "You're serious?"

She nodded. "Never more."

Damn, but she was a stubborn woman. A trait he found infinitely sexy. Usually. "You realize that the chief of detectives has to approve this."

A smile played on her lips. "I've got a special in with him." Her eyes searched his face for a sign that he wouldn't oppose her. That he was only teasing. "I don't think he'll turn me down."

"Don't be too sure."

She couldn't tell if Brian was serious or not. But he had to understand what this meant to her. It was the difference between opening up a window and letting the air come to her, and going outside.

"I need to get back on the street, Brian. I can't push another piece of paper and maintain my sanity. I'm a doer. Remember?"

He'd lost count of how many times, waking and sleeping, that he'd relived the scene, her on the ground, her blood seeping between his fingers as he tried to stop its flow. Stop her life from flowing away along with it. "All too well."

Her eyes held his for a long moment. "Don't wrap me in a cocoon or I'll smother."

But he did want to wrap her in a cocoon. Much the way she wanted to protect her children. Another impossibility. "What do your kids think about this?"

The man didn't play fair, she thought. He'd hit her in her one vulnerable spot.

"I haven't told them. They've got enough to deal with." Her words caused him to eye her quizzically. "I told Riley about the possibility of Ben being alive today, and then called a family meeting at lunch to tell the others."

"How did they take it?"

"Predictably." She raised her voice slightly as the noise level rose. "Zack seemed resigned, Taylor kept her feelings to herself and Frank…" She thought of the expression on her youngest's face as he'd digested the news. "Frank was angry."

"Angry? At who? You?"

She shook her head. She doubted very much if Frank would ever be angry with her. Their bond was too strong. "His father. For skipping out on us." She suddenly realized that the noise had abruptly stopped. The power shovel's head hung just above the hole where the casket laid, a dog looking down at the hole it had dug. "Showtime," she murmured, walking over toward the grave site.

Brian put his hand out, momentarily stopping her. She seemed confused as he motioned for his sons to take over. "Go ahead, get it out and open it."

Lila pulled her arm away. She wasn't going to have

him try to protect her. Her head high, with determined steps, Lila moved forward to the edge of the grave.

"You're going to have to move out of the way if you don't want the casket to hit you," Troy told her gently.

With a nod of her head, she stepped back. Lila held her breath as the coffin was placed on the ground beside the gaping hole. Her heart nearly stopped as the mahogany lid was lifted.

Brian shone a flashlight on the casket's occupant.

The corpse she looked down on could have been anyone. Evidence of the horrific death he had met still lingered, even after all this time.

It was no less than she'd expected.

The mortician she'd engaged for the job could only work so many miracles. Of necessity, the service had been closed casket.

Oh God, what if this really is Ben?

What if it isn't?

Rousing herself, she became aware of Dax. He laid out the long, black bag that the M.E.'s office used to transport bodies to the morgue. His brothers, Troy and Jared, lifted the body and deposited it into the body bag as best they could.

The sound of the zipper closing as the body was sealed into the black bag echoed hauntingly in her head. She drew in a long breath and released it before she turned toward Brian.

"Now what?" she asked stoically.

"Now we take the body to Patience's animal hospital." He'd put his niece on alert after making sure that this was all right with her. "She's waiting for us."

"Then let's get on with it," Lila murmured. She turned away as Jared and Troy lifted the body bag.

"This is like a ghoulish nightmare, you know that, right?" she whispered to Brian as they walked back to his car.

Behind them, Brian's sons were placing the body bag into the back of Dax's SUV.

He didn't want to dwell on the nightmare portion. It was bad enough he'd been haunted ever since he'd seen the surveillance tape. "With any luck, it'll be over with soon."

She got in on the passenger seat and shut the door. "How many days in 'soon'?"

"As few as humanly possible." Brian turned his key in the ignition, starting the engine. "I'm putting a rush on it."

Under ordinary circumstances, if the lab wasn't overloaded, DNA testing took an average of two weeks. But there were ways around that. Costly ways.

"That's going to cost extra, isn't it?" she asked. And the city was tight with its allocation of money.

"It's covered," he told her flatly, pulling away from the curb. This was coming out of his own pocket. Otherwise, there would be forms to fill out and explanations to make. He didn't want to put Lila and her family through that unless absolutely necessary.

Everything was covered. Except for the emotional turmoil this created for her and for her children.

* * *

It was a long night.

After an appropriate sample had been taken in order to conduct a proper DNA test—Lila had found an old comb that still had a few strands of Ben's hair to use as a control—the body was returned to the cemetery and placed back in its casket.

Lila insisted on being there throughout the ordeal.

"I don't know what to hope for," she said to Brian as they drove away from the cemetery for the second time that night. "Whether to hope that Ben's dead or that he's still alive." She didn't know if she could make Brian understand what she was feeling, or even if it made any sense at all. "He's the father of my children. I should be happy that there's a chance he's still alive— and yet, I don't want him to be. I want this behind me." She looked at Brian's profile as they drove through the darkened streets back to her house. "I'd moved on. I want my life back." There was pain in her voice. "Does that make me a terrible person?"

"That makes you a normal person," Brian told her. He felt for her and wished he could say something to make her feel better. "Whether Ben's alive or not, that doesn't change anything between us."

"How can you say that?" she cried, doing her best to even out her tone. "If Ben is still alive, then that means I'm a married woman."

"In name only," Brian insisted. He didn't want to lose her, especially not to someone who'd long since stopped being worthy of her. "From what you told me, he stopped being your husband long before he was killed—or thought to be killed." The light turned red and Brian eased his foot onto the brake before turning to look at her. He needed to snap her out of this. "I was serious about that party," he said out of the blue.

"Party?" she echoed, drawing a blank. Her brain was spinning around and around, trapped in a hamster wheel.

"Andrew's party this Saturday," he reminded her. "You and your family are invited and nobody is accepting excuses." He smiled, but his voice was firm.

She knew he meant well, but even though it was two days away, she wasn't up to a party. "I don't know if I can face people."

"Sure you can," he assured her. "You put on a brave front. There's an interesting thing about putting on a brave front. You do it long enough, you start to believe it's real. You stop pretending because it's become real." The light turned green and he shifted back to the gas pedal. "Personally, I think we all need a little bit of mindless fun. Besides, I already told Andrew you were all coming." He grinned. "Andrew does not take no for an answer. You don't come and I can guarantee he'll show up on your doorstep to personally *bring* you to the party."

She laughed softly, shaking her head. "You Cavanaughs are a pushy lot."

He spared her a quick look that spoke volumes. "You don't know the half of it."

Chapter 13

The dark-haired woman looked at the man standing across from her in the tiny, claustrophobic, run-down hotel room. The air was thick with a stale smell, dust and her impatience.

"What the hell is taking you so long?" she demanded. "We should be gone by now."

The dark eyes were malevolent as he turned from the window with its view of a Dumpster. He'd made it clear that the unexpected delay was not to his liking, either. But that wasn't why he was angry, she thought. Something more was at work here, something that had gotten under his skin and made him surly.

"It'll take as long as it takes," he snapped at her. There was a finality to his tone.

She already knew he didn't like being challenged. Well, too bad. She didn't like what she saw going on. "Know what I think? I think you like all this. I think you like being here." She tossed her long, straight black hair over her shoulder. Did he think she was blind? "I think you still love her."

The look in his eyes warned her to stop right there. She was too angry to listen. "You don't know what you're talking about."

The lower lip on her full mouth jutted out petulantly. She'd risked heaven and earth for this man, abandoned everything she knew in order to help him. To nurse him back to health. To be with him.

God damn him, he *owed* her. She wasn't about to watch him slip through her fingers.

Hands on her hips, she thrust her ample chest forward, a portrait of defiance. "All right, if I'm wrong, why don't you just get rid of her and get what you came for so we can finally get the hell out of here before our luck runs out?"

Steely anger, born of the sharp sting of betrayal, bubbled within his veins, threatening to spill over. He struggled to keep from hitting the small woman. He wasn't the man he used to be, but one swipe of the back of his hand could still send her flying across the room. Breaking her neck would be easier than opening up a brand-new, vacuum-packed jar of peanut butter.

"Get off my back, woman," he growled. "I do things my way and no two-bit slut is going to tell me what I should or should do."

"Two-bit slut?" Her chest heaved as she repeated the insult that had cut her to the bone. Rage slid through her veins. "Maybe I'll just go to the police, tell them what really happened three years ago. I still know some guys there. I'm sure they'd be real interested in knowing where you've been all these years." Her eyes blazed as she continued talking. "The statute of limitations hasn't run out yet. There's probably still a big reward out for any information. I don't need you for the money."

She needed him for other things, things she knew she could get from another man but only wanted from him.

"Yeah," she said slowly, hoping to goad him either into action or into abandoning his plans, at least for now, "maybe I'll do just that. Maybe I'll go to the police."

He was too fast for her.

One second he was across the room, glaring at her, the next, he was right there, beside her, his large hand beneath her throat, slamming her up against the wall with such force, it jarred her teeth.

Her breath caught and stood still in her lungs. Fear danced through her as she found herself staring up into the face of evil.

"Are you threatening me?" he demanded darkly.

She whimpered. His powerful hand had all but squeezed all the air out of her throat. Panic began to take

over. Struggling for breath, she could only form the
word "no" with her lips. No sound came out.

The next moment, as he carelessly opened his hand,
she slid down to the floor, unconscious.

"Bitch," he uttered, walking away. Hating the fact
that she was right.

"Lila McIntyre," Andrew Cavanaugh declared with
obvious pleasure. He took her hands into both of his
own, the very gesture making her feel welcomed. "It's
about time."

On his way back to the kitchen when he'd heard the
doorbell, he'd gone to answer it himself rather that call
over someone else to do it for him. Behind him, the
house was packed to the rafters with people enjoying
themselves and trying to talk above one another. It
made for a pleasant, albeit a loud, din.

Music played somewhere, a faint ribbon of a tune,
but it was all but drowned out in the wake of the raised
voices weaving through one another, forming an oddly
pleasing, cacophonous whole.

"Yes," Lila agreed, "it is."

She'd always liked Andrew, even when he was her
superior. There'd always been something genuine about
him. He had the air of a natural-born leader and his men
had been loyal to a fault.

Nothing had really changed. Even as she stood here
on the threshold, Brian beside her, she could feel the
warmth emanating from within the house. Not the

physical warmth generated from so many bodies in the same space but the emotional kind. Here were people who all genuinely liked one another. Loved one another. Even to stand on the perimeter was to feel it.

She'd tried to create that sort of atmosphere, that sort of feeling, within her own home when her children had been young. She'd been forced to pull double duty in a never ending effort to dispel the negative energy every time Ben's mood turned sour. Which had become more and more frequent as time went on.

Cocking her head, Lila looked past Andrew's broad shoulder at the gathering. The last time she'd been here, as Brian's partner, Andrew had been the struggling single father of five and the oldest had been in his teens.

"Your family's doubled," she noted.

"Tripled," he corrected with no small touch of pride. "All the kids are married now—" and by all, he meant his two nieces and four nephews, as well "—every last one of them, with kids of their own." Just then, a petite blond woman with a classically pretty face came up to join him. Andrew casually slipped his arm about her waist. "And my Rose is back." There was no missing the love that existed between the two. Lila felt herself becoming almost envious. "Just as I always knew she would be."

"How about this man?" Rose asked with a radiant smile as she rested a hand against his shoulder as if to cover his heart. "Never giving up when everyone else told him I was dead."

"You have to admit, all the evidence everyone found pointed to your having drowned in the river," Brian reminded his sister-in-law gently. That same evidence had very nearly been Andrew's undoing until he'd come around, clinging to hope that over the years was stretched thinner than a violin string. Stretched, but never broken.

Andrew nodded. It almost seemed like a bad dream now, all those years of searching.

"All the physical evidence, yes. But there's such a thing as faith of the heart. And my heart refused to believe what my brain—and everyone else—was trying to tell it."

"Don't go spreading that around," Brian advised, his expression purposely devoid of humor. "You'll give police procedure a bad name."

"Not me," Andrew laughed. Then he looked at the two people on his doorstep. They looked like a couple, he thought. Like they belonged together. He wondered if either one of them realized that. "Well, you two just going to stand there, posing for statues, or are you going to come in?"

"The very minute you step back, out of the way, brother," Brian replied amicably. "The very minute you step back."

"Always had a smart mouth on him," Andrew commented to Lila. He left his arm casually tucked around Rose's waist as he did as his younger brother asked. "By the way," he addressed Lila, "your kids are already here. A fine bunch—and top-notch officers, all of them. You should be very proud of them."

"I am," Lila assured the former police chief.

For a moment her gaze swept over the crowd as she searched for the familiar faces of her own brood, wondering if any of them had brought dates. Probably not, she judged. None of them was in a serious relationship. Taylor had been, but that had abruptly ended and so far, her older daughter wasn't talking about it.

The vast number of people she saw all but overwhelmed Lila. It looked as if there were close to fifty—if not more—in the immediate vicinity.

"Are all of these actually relatives of yours?" she asked in disbelief.

"Hey, Dad," Rayne, Andrew's youngest daughter, popped her head out of the entrance to the kitchen and called out his name. "I just walked by the oven and something dinged at me." When he made no immediate response, she cupped her mouth and repeated her statement, this time a decibel louder.

Andrew waved his hand to indicate that he'd heard her. "I'll be right there," he all but shouted. Turning his head back to Brian and Lila, he grinned. "I'm surprised she even recognizes an oven," he confided to Lila, then pretended to sigh. "Can hardly work a can opener. The girl doesn't take after me at all."

"I don't know about that," Rose countered. "I hear Rayne's a great detective." She beamed at her husband. "That makes her just like you."

"Better than him," Brian interjected.

"I don't recall anyone asking for your opinion," Andrew said to his brother.

Rose rolled her eyes and then glanced toward Lila. "They never grow up." And then she waved her husband toward the kitchen. "Shoo. Go rescue whatever's calling to you."

"Yes, ma'am," Andrew replied meekly, pretending to salute her.

Turning toward her brother-in-law and the woman he'd brought with him, Rose smiled. "Can I get either of you two anything?"

"Don't stand on formality," Andrew called back, overhearing. "They can get their own 'anything.' Brian knows where everything is. God knows he's made himself at home often enough." Though worded like a veiled criticism, it wasn't anything of the kind. Andrew liked nothing better than to have his clan gather together at his house—with or without an occasion.

"You heard the man." Rose gestured toward the buffet table that had been set up against one wall. It ran from one wall to the other and its entire length was covered with different servings of meat, vegetables and desserts that could make anyone watching their weight weep with frustration. "Help yourselves."

"Rose!" Andrew's disembodied voice summoned her to join him in the kitchen.

"Coming, master."

With a grin, Rose winked at her two newest guests

and then turned on her heel. Elbowing her way through the throng, she went toward the kitchen and disappeared.

"Why don't we do what the lady suggested?" Brian urged. "As I recall, the one time you were here, it wasn't for a meal." Lila nodded. "Well, I'd never say this in front of him, but you're in for a treat. Andrew was a great cop. He's an even better chef."

"It smells wonderful," she agreed as Brian took hold of her arm and began to guide her toward the food-laden table.

Although people stepped out of their way, it was still tough going. Every time she made eye contact, the other person would nod, as if they already knew her. Andrew had been interrupted before he had a chance to answer her question.

She asked it again, this time of Brian. "Are all these people really related to you or was Andrew just pulling my leg?"

"No leg pulling," Brian assured her as they reached journey's end. He picked up a large, laminated paper plate and began filling it with servings from different dishes and pans. "Every last one of these people is a Cavanaugh, or married to a Cavanaugh. Except, of course," he qualified, "for your kids."

"Even the children?" There were several managing to play what looked like a game of tag just beyond the table. No less than five more, slightly older, crowded around an entertainment center. On the screen was a chubby mouse trying to educate a thin, hungry-looking alley cat. And the cat looked interested in eating his teacher.

"Even the children."

Watching her over his shoulder, Brian sounded amused at her disbelief. Lila shook her head at his answer. "Go forth and be fruitful and multiply," she murmured under her breath, paraphrasing a biblical passage.

Because of all the noise, she'd thought that her remark would go unheard but the man preparing a plate in front of her had to be part bat. He'd heard and he was now grinning.

"That's almost the best part," Brian told her, bringing his lips down to her ear so that she could hear him. "Being fruitful and multiplying."

She not only heard him, but she also reacted to him. Not to his words exactly but to the breath it took to say them. She felt it, warm along her neck, creating goose bumps up and down her arms as well as a head-spinning anticipation. Lila had a sudden, overpowering and totally irresistible urge to kiss him. Only extreme self-control allowed her to successfully rein in that impulse.

"Almost?" she echoed hoarsely. If she kept him talking, maybe he wouldn't notice that she was turning into a mass of lust.

He nodded.

"And what's better?" she asked.

"That's easy," he told her, retiring a ladle back into the large tureen filled with deceptively innocent-looking mashed potatoes. He knew for a fact they gave new meaning to the word spicy. "Seeing the end result of all that multiplying." He grinned at her, thinking of his own children. "Can't beat that."

He loved his children. Why did she find that so hopelessly sexy? Maybe because Ben always seemed so indifferent to theirs. As she looked back, she recalled how he'd taken very little interest in his kids, even when things were still going his way. His own world, his own problems, always took precedence over anything the children went through. He never actually saw them as full-fledged human beings. In the end, only he mattered.

You missed so much, Ben.

"No," she agreed as Brian handed her the plate he'd just put together for her, "you can't." Lila glanced down at the plate. There seemed to be a little bit of everything on it. Her own individual smorgasbord. "What is all this?"

"Heaven on a decorated paper plate," Taylor answered, coming up behind her. "Hi, Chief." Her greeting was accompanied by a wide grin before she looked back at her mother. "You have *got* to try that," she insisted, pointing to an exotic-looking appetizer nestled between a dollop of spicy potatoes and something that involved an avocado. "No offense, Mom, but Chief Cavanaugh cooks rings around you. That Chief Cavanaugh," she added as an afterthought, nodding toward the kitchen when she realized that the man beside her mother also answered to that title.

"No offense taken," Lila assured her.

The moment she slipped the appetizer between her lips, she felt as if she was on the cusp of an experience she'd never had before. Taking a deep breath, Lila chewed very slowly, almost in slow motion, savoring every last morsel as it slid seductively down the length of her throat.

Her eyes widened in appreciation and surprise. "I think I'm in love," she pronounced as the last bit found its way to her stomach. She glanced over to see if there was more and if she'd seem too greedy if she took another—or three. Her eyes shifted to Brian. "Where did he learn how to *do* this?" she asked. The men she knew didn't cook. If they were lucky, they knew how to warm prepared meals in a microwave.

As far as Brian knew, no special training or classes were involved. It was just a natural gift, born of interest and necessity.

"Andrew always had a knack for cooking," he told her. "Back in the day, he put himself through school working in one restaurant after another. Two restaurants when he got married and the kids started coming. That was before he joined the force. When he left to take care of his family after Rose disappeared, I kept trying to get him to open his own place but he said he wasn't interested in cooking for strangers on a regular basis. He just liked feeding his family. It's his own personal way of keeping everyone together," Brian told her as he put together a plate for himself. "He's been holding command breakfasts for what feels like years now."

"Command breakfasts," she echoed. As she said them, the words struck a chord. "I've heard about them."

"You're invited, you know."

Lila turned around to find that Andrew had managed to materialize behind her. The senior Cavanaugh was holding a tray of plump, tiny, golden-brown squares he'd just taken from the oven. He moved the tray closer to her, silently offering her a sample.

"To breakfast," he explained in case she hadn't followed his meaning. Glancing toward Brian, he instructed, "Bring her next time you come. I trust that'll be soon."

Brian exchanged glances with Lila. "You'll have to excuse my brother. He still thinks he's the chief of police."

Andrew's expression gave no indication of the humor that was just beneath. "I am." Either way, there was no arguing with his tone. As Brian had warned earlier, Andrew didn't accept the word no.

He raised the tray a little higher and closer to her. "Take one," he urged Lila.

As she reached for one of the tempting squares with its heavenly aroma, hands seemed to magically emerge all around her, reaching every which way to snare one of the prizes off the tray that Andrew held between oven-mittened hands.

"Vultures," he declared, but Andrew grinned from ear to ear as he said it.

Another bit of heaven, Lila thought the moment she'd popped the converted square into her mouth and sampled it. This tasted too good not to carry serious consequences.

"I'm going to gain five pounds before I leave here, aren't I?" Lila asked Brian, wiping her fingertips delicately across a napkin she was holding in the same hand.

"At the very least," Brian agreed, getting out of the way as more people crowded around the swiftly depleting tray. "But that's okay." His eyes swept over her. "An extra few pounds'll look good on you."

Taylor was about to move away to give someone else access to the tray. She seemed to overhear Brian's comment. Her mouth curved as she looked over her shoulder at her mother. Bending her head, she whispered into her ear, "You're blushing."

Lila drew herself up. "I am not."

"Am not what?" Brian asked, standing on her other side.

"Eating too much." It was the first thing that popped into Lila's mind as she willed the bright color from her face to no avail. She could *feel* the blush making its way up her cheeks. "Taylor seems to think that she's my conscience."

Sparing her a glance, Brian merely smiled to himself, as if he knew better but, being a gentleman, he kept it to himself and allowed her the fabrication.

Chapter 14

Lila sat back as she secured the seat belt around her. Darkness had long since enveloped the world outside the passenger window. A sigh of contentment escaped her lips even as traces of exuberance within her continued.

"Is that a good sigh or a bad one?" Brian asked, engaging the engine. Was she happy to be leaving, or just happy?

"A good one." She glanced at his profile. Her contentment grew. "I can't remember when I'd had a better time."

Jockeying out of the parking place, Brian carefully guided his car away from the others and onto the street.

The only bad thing about these gatherings was the lack of space outside Andrew's house. There were vehicles parked all up and down the long block and across the street.

"I can," Brian replied, sparing her a significant look.

As if they had a single mind between them, she knew exactly what he was referring to. Their lovemaking. "At a party," she qualified.

She could almost see his eyes twinkling as he smiled. "As I recall, we made our own party."

The man was incorrigible. Lila laughed, feeling lighter than she had in years. So light that she could practically float away.

She had all but forgotten what it felt like to socialize, to mingle among people whose company she really enjoyed and who enjoyed hers. She'd all but been in exile until today.

That had been of her own doing, she reminded herself. First because Ben had made her leave the force to be a full-time mother. Once she had, he'd very effectively cut her out of the professional portion of his life. And second, because after Ben's death, when the rumors and suspicions about Ben had begun to make the rounds, she'd isolated herself in order to cope. In order to avoid the pain that the whispered suspicions caused her.

Back then, she'd felt she owed it to Ben to defend his name. Now she realized that she'd wasted a great deal of time because of a foolish misplaced sense of loyalty.

Ben had been her emotional jailer and she owed him nothing. Today had shown her just how much she'd missed by subscribing to a completely wrong philosophy.

"All right," she allowed, not bothering to suppress her grin, "the most fun I'd had in a long time with my clothes on."

Slowing for a yellow light, Brian reached over and lightly squeezed her knee. It was a hopelessly intimate gesture, signifying just how many barriers between them had been done away with.

"Better." The light was green and he returned his other hand to the steering wheel. "Your kids blended in well with the group."

Brian hoped the comment sounded as casual as he tried to make it. He didn't want to spook her and make her retreat. All evening, he'd kept an eye on her four kids, watching them interact with his family. Like Andrew, family had always been his first priority. It was very important to him that her family got along with his.

He was aware that the McIntyres already knew the Cavanaughs. Acquaintances went all the way back to when he and Lila had been first partnered. However, a lot of time had passed since then. People changed, values shifted. But from what he'd observed tonight, Zack, Taylor, Riley and Frank could just as easily been his as hers. And that mattered.

He saw pleasure whisper along her face as she smiled and nodded in response. "Yes, they did, didn't they?" Obviously he hadn't been the only one watching the McIntyres interact with the Cavanaughs. "I'm hoping your family's example rubs off on mine."

The comment seemed to have come out of the blue and he was clueless as to what she meant by that. "Come again?"

"They're all married." Something, she was sure, he took for granted. "Your kids, Andrew's kids and Mike's, too. They've all found someone they want to spend the rest of their lives with and most of them have started families."

At times, she was certain that none of hers would do that, that they would all lead solitary lives, no children, no spouses, not even a significant other in the mix. And that, ultimately, was her fault. Her marriage had set a bad precedent for them. She should have left Ben a long time ago.

"Sometimes I worry that the example they saw while growing up will keep mine from even considering marriage, which means that they'll never discover just how good it can be." God knew that she had never been privy to that on her own.

Lila caught her lower lip between her teeth. She felt a little self-conscious, baring her soul this way. Brian probably wondered why she'd put up with Ben all those years, why she'd married him in the first place. She didn't want him thinking she was one of those clingy women who stoically put up with being abused, afraid to venture out on her own. It wasn't fear that had held her in place, it was love. And hope that Ben would return to his senses and be the man she'd originally fallen in love with.

Hope that ultimately led nowhere.

"It was good, you know," she said softly as they drove to her house. "My marriage. In the beginning, it was good. I don't even know why it started falling apart." She shrugged, helpless even now to pinpoint when it had all begun to change, to unravel. "If I did, maybe I could have fixed it."

He hated seeing her blame herself. "You tried your best," Brian told her firmly. "You're not to blame. Ben was."

"You can't know that."

Oh, but he did. He'd stake his life on it. "I know you."

That made one of them, Lila thought. These days, she hardly knew herself. Or was it the old Lila, Ben's wife, that she didn't know? Nothing seemed clear anymore. "I've changed."

He shook his head, standing by his statement. "You can't change goodness, Lila. For all his attributes and talents, Ben McIntyre was an insecure man." He slanted a look at her before focusing back at the road. She had to know this, he reasoned. "He didn't force you to leave the force because he wanted your children to have a full-time mother, he made you leave because your being amid mostly men just made his insecurities that much bigger and harder to deal with."

Lila opened her mouth to deny it, but couldn't. "Maybe you're right."

There was no "maybe" about it. "You know I am, Lila."

Leaning her head back against the headrest, Lila closed her eyes. The threat of her present situation held her prisoner. As its hold tightened around her, the heady, euphoric effects of the party began to slip away.

"What do I do, Brian?" She opened her eyes again, staring off into the darkness. "What do I do if that body in the casket doesn't turn out to be Ben? What do I do if he's alive?"

He knew what he wanted to tell her, but it wasn't fair. She needed to come to that conclusion herself, without prodding. "What do you want to do?"

There was no hesitation. The words shot out like bullets. "Divorce him."

Silently, Brian congratulated himself. Score one for his team. He did what he could to contain his feeling of triumph. This couldn't be easy for her. "Then do it."

She laughed softly to herself at the irony of it all. The day that Ben's body washed up on the shore, she'd gone to a lawyer to see about obtaining a divorce. Somehow, they seemed to have come full circle.

A headache formed across the front of her skull. She ran a hand over her forehead, willing it to fade away. "When did life get so complicated?"

"It's always been complicated," Brian contradicted, then spared her a quick look. Her profile looked soft in the darkness and he could feel a pull within him. Could feel himself wanting her. "But some things are still simple."

She couldn't think of a single thing. "Oh, yeah? Like what?"

"Like love." The two words and the sentiment they conveyed lit her up.

But he was wrong there, she thought, wishing he wasn't. "Oh no, love's the most complicated part of it all." Caring for him had complicated her life.

The car eased to a stop in the driveway. They'd arrived at her house. Cutting off the engine, Brian made no move to get out of the vehicle. Instead he left the keys in the ignition and turned toward her.

For a moment, there was nothing but silence in the car.

Brian gently feathered his fingertips along her face, feeling his own pulse quickening. How had he managed to keep his hands off her all these years? To allow such distance? Now that he'd made love to her, no way could he walk away. He wanted her and was willing to accept any terms she wanted to dictate. As long as she was his.

"It doesn't have to be," he told her, his voice all but seducing her. "Stripped down to its bare essence, it becomes very simple. You either love someone or you don't."

She'd already used the "L" word, already told him that she loved him. Her part in this was decided. It was his turn.

"And?" she asked so quietly, her voice almost faded away. "What's the verdict?"

Even as the words emerged, Lila couldn't believe she was asking him that. And yet, this was Brian, the Brian she'd once known better than she'd known herself. The Brian she knew she could say anything to, could trust with any secret.

But could she trust him with her heart?

Love, and fear of love, did funny things to people. It changed them, not always for the better. She only had to remember Ben to know that.

Lila held her breath as the silence inside the car slowly stretched out, its two ends melting into the darkness.

His eyes held hers. "I think you know."

But Lila slowly moved her head from side to side, her eyes still pinned by his. As was her soul. She needed to hear it.

"No, I don't."

She had to know how he felt. Of that Brian was utterly certain. But she needed the words, needed to hear him say them. He understood that. It wasn't that they weren't there. He'd just kept them hidden for so long. He had a hard time raising them, exposing them again. It was time to stop hiding.

"I have loved you, Lila, for a very long time." Now that he'd finally told her, he had to tell her the entire truth. "I didn't want to at first and I never really intended to admit to it. Not to you. Not even to myself. You were married and had a family—and so did I. But that didn't change how I felt about you. And now things are finally different." Now there was hope.

Lila pressed her lips together as she shook her head. "I still might be married."

"In name only," he reminded her. He took a breath. It was time to take the plunge. "I loved you then, I love you now and any time you're ready, Lila, I want you to marry me."

Her eyes widened. Was it really that much of a surprise for her? He'd been raised to believe that when you loved someone, really loved them, you married them. He still believed that.

"I'm not rushing you," he said gently. "I've waited this long, I can wait a while longer. All I ask is that you don't make me wait forever." That being said, he opened his door and got out. Circling the vehicle, he came around to her side and opened the door. He took her hand and helped her out. "I'm not coming over tonight," he told her. "You've got a lot to think about and you probably want to be alone."

His understanding almost undid her.

God, but he was good to her. He was so intuitive of her feelings, it was almost as if they shared the same mind. She should be shouting "yes" from the rooftops, but he was right, she did need time. Time to sort everything out. Time to savor the proposal.

"I do love you, Brian."

He smiled at her. "I know." And he could wait, he told himself. Because the promise of forever hung in the balance. He nodded toward her house. "I'll go in with you to check out the house." He saw her begin to protest but he was ready for her. "Two sets of eyes are better than one."

So she unlocked the door and went with him from room to room, flipping on the lights, scanning each area carefully. Except for Duchess, the house was empty and everything was where she'd left it. Nothing had been disturbed.

Threading her arms through his, she walked Brian back to the front door. Her heart was close to bursting, and she felt conflicted. How would all this work out?

Brian opened the front door again and then paused on the other side of the threshold. The look in his eyes melted her.

"Thanks for being so understanding." She'd never meant anything so heartily in her life.

Brian brushed his lips against hers, purposely holding his body rigid so that their lips were their only point of contact. "That's what I'm here for." He deliberately banked down the ache in his chest. "I'll call you tomorrow."

Lila nodded. "Tomorrow." She'd give him his answer tomorrow, she promised silently. But tonight, she just wanted a little time to herself.

She watched him walk back to his car and then closed the door because she knew that he wouldn't leave until she did.

Lila leaned against the door, suddenly exhausted. Was she crazy not screaming "yes" to his proposal and jumping into his arms? It was what she really wanted to do. Brian would never hurt her the way Ben had. What was she afraid of?

And then she knew, perhaps had known from the beginning. She was afraid of having it all fall apart on her. Despite how perfect the situation seemed, how perfect Brian seemed, she was afraid of everything crumbling like a house of cards.

Because once upon a time, Ben had seemed perfect, too.

Her headache grew.

She couldn't think about this now. Maybe tomorrow, after a good night's sleep, she could sort it all out and put her fears to rest once and for all.

Instead of the bedroom, Lila changed direction and walked into to the kitchen. Whenever she felt stressed, she drank a glass of warm milk. It was old-fashioned and her kids had teased her about it more than once, but for her this remedy worked. At least it had in the past. With any luck, it would work again, she thought, opening the refrigerator.

When he pulled away from her house, Brian began to head for home. Halfway down the second block, he changed his mind and made a U-turn. Home could wait.

He was far too restless to go to sleep anytime soon. Too many things were running around in his mind. Rather than head home, he found himself driving toward the precinct on the outside chance that the DNA test had come through early and that the lab tech had an answer for him. He knew he was pushing things, that even a rush job took longer than he was happy about, but sometimes the stars all aligned themselves and all went according to plan.

At least he could hope.

Less than one third the usual number of cars were in the precinct parking lot at this hour. Because of recent budget cuts, the night shift had been scaled back, as had the number of people who worked in the crime investigation unit. But a few people were still working and all he needed was one overzealous lab technician to make his day—or night, Brian amended, looking up at the dark sky as he ascended the steps to the precinct.

The sergeant behind the information desk seemed surprised to see him. Until this moment, except for a handful of non-emergency calls, it had been a very quiet night. The sergeant, a twelve-year veteran, was alert. "Something wrong, Chief?" she asked.

He shook his head. No point in saying anything until *all* the facts were in. "Just wanted to check on something, Cynthia."

The brunette nodded, and he made his way to the elevators.

Rather than go up to his office, Brian went down to the basement where the crime scene investigation labs were located.

At that time of night, there was very little traffic. His footsteps echoed in his ears as he walked down the long hallway to the tech lab where he'd dropped off the DNA sample.

Only one technician was on duty, but it had come to his attention that Nathan Sinclair, an overachiever since he was five, was worth at least three regular technicians. He lived and breathed the department and no one knew their way around the equipment the way he did. It was Nathan he'd given the samples to in the first place.

Stopping in the doorway, Brian glanced in. Bent over a report, Nathan had his back to him.

Brian didn't bother with a greeting. Entering, he asked, "Anything?"

Nathan looked at him and instantly his sparse mouth stretched into a smile. Brian recognized triumph when he saw it and banked down a wave of excitement.

"Just came in over the wire in the last ten minutes," Nathan told him. "I was just about to call you, as per your orders," he added to cover himself. "I made this my priority."

"I appreciate it." Brian thanked him because it was expected and after his hard work, Nathan deserved to hear it. However, his entire focus was on the question he asked next. The question that had risen up like a living, breathing entity ever since he'd first looked at the surveillance tape from the bargain store. "What's the result?"

"You buried the wrong man," Nathan told him simply. "I don't know yet who you did bury, but it's definitely not Ben McIntyre."

Brian knew that Lila had given them a few strands of Ben's hair with the follicles still attached, but he wanted to be absolutely certain. "You're sure?"

Nathan raised his right hand as if he were in court, taking a solemn oath. "Never more sure of anything in my life."

He needed to tell Lila. "Great job," Brian said, already on his way out.

"You want me to try to find out who you did bury?" Nathan asked, as if searching for a new challenge.

Taking out his cell phone, Brian pressed the single key that would connect him to Lila's landline. "I'd appreciate it."

"You got it," Nathan called after him.

Brian hardly heard him. Striding down the hall back to the bank of elevators, he frowned. The phone on the other end just kept ringing. Lila wasn't picking up. She had several extensions throughout the house so she was bound to hear one of them no matter what room she was in.

Unless she'd gone out, he thought suddenly.

Why would she go out? She been dead on her feet.

Nervousness flared through his veins like unharnessed lightning.

Ben wasn't dead. What if…?

Brian hit the key he'd assigned to her cell phone. It went to voice mail after three rings.

Something was definitely wrong.

Cursing under his breath, a sense of urgency pervading him, Brian ran past the elevators and hurried to the stairs instead.

He took them two at a time.

"Chief?" Cynthia asked as she saw him all but burst through the door and fly by the desk to the front doors.

"Send a patrol car to Lila McIntyre's house, 1232 Hamilton Street," he rattled off, sparing her the need to look up the address.

Cynthia knew better than to ask why. Picking up the phone, she called the dispatch officer.

Damn it, Brian cursed himself, hurrying down the steps to his car. Why hadn't he insisted on staying with her tonight? Why had he opted to give her space? She didn't need space, she needed to be safe.

The empty streets whizzed by him as he drove, praying it wasn't too late.

Chapter 15

The moment Brian turned onto the street, he saw the flames.

Lila's house was on fire.

Because it was still localized on one side of the first floor, from the looks of it, the fire had just begun. In the distance, Brian was vaguely aware of the sounds of approaching sirens.

He didn't have time to wait for help.

After parking in the driveway, Brian bolted up the lawn to the front of the house. The door was locked. Banging on it with his fist brought no response from within, except for the sound of Duchess, barking. Mercifully, he didn't feel any heat along the wood.

That meant the fire hadn't made its way across the whole floor.

Yet.

Within thirty seconds of his arrival, Brian stripped off his jacket, wrapped it along his arm and smashed through the living room window. Not wasting any time clearing away the remaining glass, he dove in.

Jagged pieces scraped against his skin. The smell of smoke was everywhere, but he was right. The flames hadn't reached this part of the house yet.

"Lila! Lila, where are you?" There was no response. He called out her name again with the same results.

Duchess came to the head of the stairs, barking urgently.

"She's upstairs, isn't she?" he called to the dog. Duchess turned on her heels and ran back to Lila's room. Brian ran up the stairs, two at a time. Out of the corner of his eye, he could see flames coming out of the kitchen. He didn't have much time.

Heart pounding, Brian reached her room. The door was open. Lila lay in bed, sound asleep from all appearances. Why didn't she wake up when Duchess began to bark? Losing no time, he crossed the room and shook Lila by the shoulder.

"Lila, wake up! Wake up! The house is on fire."

Neither the words nor his shaking managed to wake her. For all intents and purposes, Lila seemed dead to the world.

Panic materialized on the perimeter of his consciousness.

Running into the bathroom, Brian soaked one of the towels in water. He doubled back and threw it over Lila's face just before he pulled her out of the bed. She never stirred, but he could feel her chest rising and falling. At least she was still alive. He wasn't too late.

The smoke began to fill the air. Breathing was becoming a challenge. Brian picked Lila up into his arms. "Follow me," he ordered the dog.

Duchess did just that, shadowing his footsteps as he made his way down the stairs as quickly as he could.

The heat seemed all around them, but the flames had not yet caught up. It was only a matter of minutes, if that. The flames had multiplied, leaching out of the kitchen and swiftly working through the first floor. He was aware that his lungs were bursting by the time he reached the bottom of the stairs.

Lila wasn't stirring, and he was afraid of why.

By the time he'd made it through the front door, he gasped for breath. The dog was barking louder than ever. The sweet smell of air as he filled his lungs was all but overwhelming. Coughing, gasping, he drew it in as quickly as possible.

His heart pounded so hard, he was sure it would crack one of his ribs. The second he'd emerged, he saw that squad cars now littered the street. More sirens echoed in the night, growing louder as they heralded the approach of fire trucks.

Brian dropped to his knees, still holding Lila.

"I'll take her, Chief," someone behind him volunteered, but Brian shook his head, afraid of backing away from her. Afraid of losing her. "Look after the dog," he ordered.

Placing Lila on the grass, he began giving her CPR until a coughing fit got in his way.

And then he felt hands on his shoulders, gently but firmly moving him aside. The next moment, a paramedic had taken his place, giving Lila CPR.

Someone tapped Brian on the shoulder. "Come with me to the ambulance," the man's partner said.

Brian couldn't tear his eyes away from the prone figure on the grass as the first paramedic did compressions on Lila's chest. Duchess pranced around her mistress, clearly distressed.

"I can't leave her," he protested.

"It's just a few steps, Chief." Gently, the paramedic urged him over to the rear of the ambulance. Firemen and hoses snaked across the lawn now, with geysers of water crashing down on the flames. "You won't be leaving her," the man reassured him.

For the next several minutes Brian felt like someone frozen in the moment. The back doors of the ambulance were open and he sat on the edge, holding an oxygen mask to his face and taking in deep breaths. He was hardly aware of what he was doing. All his attention was focused on the woman still on the ground. And then, despite all the din, above Duchess's barking, he heard it. Heard Lila cough. She was alive!

But still unconscious.

Unable to stay still any longer, Brian let the oxygen mask drop beside him, threw off the blanket from his shoulders and quickly made his way back to Lila.

"Is she going to be all right?" he demanded of the paramedic still working over her. Duchess looked up at him with the same question echoed in her brown eyes.

The man nodded, retiring the stethoscope he'd just used, leaving it hanging around his neck. "Her heart's strong."

The older of the two paramedics guided a gurney over toward Lila. "We need to take her to the hospital. I think she's just suffering from too much smoke inhalation, but we can't be sure."

Brian shook his head. It wasn't that. "When I arrived, there was hardly any smoke upstairs." There had to be another reason why he hadn't been able to wake her.

The paramedic who'd been working over her rose to his feet. "It's not smoke inhalation," he said as he helped his partner place her on the gurney. "She appears to have been sedated."

"Sedated?" Brian echoed, saying the word as if it belonged in a foreign language.

Snapping the legs of the gurney into place, the two men guided it to the back of the ambulance. The paramedic talking to Brian nodded. "Do you know if she takes sleeping pills or tranquilizers?"

Brain shook his head. "She doesn't believe in them." She'd told him that all it took to put her out was a warm glass of milk. That didn't sound like someone who would resort to sleeping pills.

"Well, maybe she changed her religion," the younger one commented. "Because I'm pretty sure she took some tonight."

Or someone slipped them to her, Brian thought, looking around. An icy feeling raked down his spine as the thought penetrated.

The street filled with Lila's neighbors, drawn by the sound of sirens and the commotion. Brian scanned the faces in the crowd quickly, convinced that Ben was responsible for this. Yet he still had no explanation as to why the man was trying to spook Lila, and then, when that hadn't worked, switched gears to smoke her out. Was this some sort of demented revenge on Ben's part?

He had no answers and that frustrated the hell out of him.

Except for her next-door neighbor, the faces he saw were unfamiliar to him. The one thing he did know was that Ben was not among them.

The paramedics placed Lila inside the ambulance. As they began to close the door, Brian put his hand in the way to stop them.

"We need to take her in, Chief," the head paramedic told him politely.

"I'm not trying to stop you," Brian explained. "But I am coming with you."

Neither paramedic felt up to arguing with the chief of detectives.

"Wait one second," Brian instructed. He waved to the next-door neighbor. "Alice, would you watch Duchess for Lila?"

The woman seemed more than happy to be of some use. "Don't give it another thought, just be with Lila," she urged.

Brian nodded, not saying anything. He rode to the hospital holding Lila's hand and praying.

Lila never opened her eyes.

She was aware of spinning. Was the room spinning?

Why? Was there an earthquake? She'd experienced earthquakes before, especially that large one in San Francisco more than a decade ago. But then things had rocked and swayed, they hadn't spun.

Prying her eyes open after several attempts, Lila realized it wasn't the room that was spinning, but her head. Spinning and hurting and making everything seem very, very fuzzy.

Where was she?

Bright sunlight streamed into the unfamiliar room. Daylight. Blinking, she tried to sit up and the enormous headache all but consumed her. For the moment, the pain flattened her.

The headache was so bad her teeth hurt.

Gingerly, Lila drew in a long breath. And then she saw him. Brian. Slumped in a chair, his eyes shut, he appeared to be sleeping.

Was this some sort of strange dream?

If it was, why did her head feel as if a marching band had just held an all-night, marathon rehearsal in it, complete with fiery batons?

"Brian?" The first time she attempted to say his name, only her lips moved, but no sound came out. She tried again, this time with moderate success. The third time his name was audible.

His eyes opened instantly. In less than a quarter of a heartbeat, he was on his feet beside her. Worry furrowed his brow, but he smiled encouragingly and took her hand in his. "How are you feeling?"

"Like somebody turned me inside out." She placed a hand to her throbbing forehead. "I can't seem to focus my mind." Lila searched his face, hoping for answers. "Where am I?"

"The hospital."

Relief blew through him like a cool wind across the night desert. She was going to be all right. All night, he'd tortured himself with the thought of what could have happened—would have happened—had he not followed his gut instinct and gone to her place.

"Hospital?" she repeated incredulously. "What am I doing here?"

"It's a long story." He wasn't going to tax her with the truth, not until she was strong enough. He held her hand a little tighter. "Lila, did you take anything last night?"

Confusion entered her eyes as she tried to make sense of the question. "Take anything?"

"Yes," he nodded. "Like sleeping pills or a tranquilizer?"

"No," she denied vehemently, her confusion growing. He knew better than that. Even when she'd been shot, she tried to refrain from taking painkillers because they made her head feel so fuzzy.

Fuzzy.

The way she felt right now.

Thoughts began to hook up in her head.

Her breath caught in her throat. "I had a glass of milk like I always do," she told him, the words rushing out after one another. "It tasted a little funny." Lila raised her eyes to his face. "Did someone do something to my milk—?"

There was no point in keeping the information from her. The toxicology test the hospital ran on her clearly pointed to her having ingested at least two of the stronger prescription sleeping pills. He knew she wouldn't have done it by choice.

"You were drugged, Lila." He had to tell her at least part of it. But in his opinion, she'd gone through too much for him to tell her the full story just yet. "Whoever's been harassing you must have gotten in and either drugged the carton of milk, or at least the glass of milk you drank." Since the kitchen had burned, there was no way to verify his theory but he believed it just the same.

Anger at the violation smothered her feelings of vulnerability. "What do they want?" she cried.

"We haven't figured that part out yet," Brian confessed.

She knew him inside and out, despite the long gap that had transpired between her leaving the force and her seeking him out. "There's something more, isn't there?"

Brian paused, sincerely debating how much he should reveal. After a beat, he told her only what she needed to know immediately.

"Someone set fire to the house." He saw her mouth drop open as she stared at him in shock. "The fire department saved most of it," he assured her quickly. "Only the kitchen and part of the family room were destroyed."

But she only heard one thing. That the fire had been deliberately set. "Someone tried to kill me?"

He hated not being able to shield her, hated having to expose her to something so brutal. Dealing with the underbelly of life on a day-to-day basis was one thing. Having it spill over into your personal life was quite another.

"Looks that way," he answered grimly, then added quickly, "look, the second they release you, you're coming home with me."

Her shoulders locked rigidly and Brian was infinitely familiar with the pose she struck. Lila, being stubborn. "I'm not going into hiding."

Another time, he might have indulged her, might have let her talk, but he'd come too close to losing her. That was not about to happen again.

"Lila, there is no arguing," he told her firmly. "I won't have you sitting in your house with a target on your body."

She knew that tone. She was going to have to let him wind down before she could convince him to let up. And then a thought hit her out of nowhere. The last thing she remembered was crawling into bed. The gap between there and here was huge.

"Who rescued me?" she asked.

"I did," he said simply. He had his story in place about how he'd called to ask her something and began to worry when she didn't answer. She didn't need to know about the lab's DNA findings just yet.

Lila started to ask how he'd happened to have been in the right place at the right time when the door to her room suddenly opened. Zack, Taylor, Riley and Frank all burst in together, talking at once. Brian moved aside to give them room.

For now, he thought, somewhat relieved, their conversation was tabled. The cavalry had arrived.

Lila insisted on going back to work the next day. He let her win the argument, but not the one that involved her going back to her house, even for a few minutes. Instead, he brought her back to his house again, telling her that anything she needed, he could pick up for her. Used to independence, she bristled at that.

Brian remained steadfast. Lila gave in—for the time being, she underscored.

"Good enough for me," he told her.

They had supper and quiet conversation. But when Lila suggested that they watch an old favorite movie running on one of the cable stations, Brian surprised her with his answer.

"I'd love to, Lila, but I can't. I've got to go out again."

Lila stared at him, stunned. "You're going out?" she demanded as he crossed to the front door.

"Just for a while," he assured her. He was confident that she would be safe here. Especially since he'd asked Jared to keep an eye on the house for him. "I've got an off-the-clock meeting with someone from the D.E.A."

She was immediately alert. The D.E.A. had been involved in the operation that had gone all wrong and supposedly gotten Ben and his partner killed. "Is it about Ben?"

He wanted to keep her safe. And the only way he had a prayer of accomplishing that was by capturing a man who was supposed to have died over three years ago. That meant lying to her. He tried to keep it down to a minimum and hoped that she'd forgive him when she finally found out.

"I can't talk about it yet." That much was true. "As soon as I can, I will," he promised her. He paused to take her into his arms. "Why don't you give one of your kids a call, have them come over to keep you company?"

She resented the fact that he thought she needed a keeper. She'd been caught napping once, it wouldn't happen again. "I'm not some invalid, Brian. Please don't treat me like one."

In her place, he'd probably react the same way. But he wasn't in her place, and he'd move heaven and earth to make sure nothing happened to her. "Invalids aren't the only ones who like company," he told her evenly. "I hear mothers like it, too."

He was right, she thought. She was acting like a shrew. "I'm sorry, I'm just edgy," she apologized. "Have you heard any news about the DNA?"

It took everything he had not to avoid her eyes. They would have given away the truth.

"Not yet." He hated lying but he knew her. If he told her the truth, that the man in Ben's coffin wasn't Ben, then she'd make the same assumptions he had. And she'd want to go with him because she'd immediately guess that he wasn't meeting anyone from the D.E.A.

And he wasn't. He was planning on staking out her place. He was positive all this had something to do with the house. All the pieces pointed toward getting her out and keeping her out. Why?

He could only come to one conclusion. If he was right, then Ben would go back to the house until he got what he wanted. Now that she had finally vacated the premises, nothing stopped Ben.

And he didn't want Lila anywhere near the house when Ben came back.

Resigned, Lila sighed. "Will you be gone long?"

He lingered at the door. "Hard to say. You know these D.E.A. types, they don't always show when they say they will. I might have to wait for him."

Lila nodded, familiar with the breed. She threaded her arms around his neck, "Give me a call if you're going to be very late." Rising on her toes, she brushed her lips against his cheek, loving him more than she could ever say. "Stay safe."

"Always," he promised. "And call someone. I'd feel better if I knew you weren't alone." He hesitated, debating on whether or not to tell her that Jared would be watching over her. He decided to gauge her reaction first. "If you don't want to call one of them, I can have one of my sons—"

Lila cut him off. "Not to worry," No way was she going to inconvenience one of his family with a baby-sitting detail. "I'll call Zack or Taylor, or maybe the whole bunch."

"Even better," he told her with a smile.

He'd already released her and was on his way out the door when he doubled back, took her into his arms and kissed her again, long and hard.

"Wow," she breathed as she tried to get her bearings once he drew back. Her bones were melting. "Is that supposed to hold me until you get back?"

"No," he told her honestly, "that's supposed to hold me until I get back. I love you."

And then he left before she could say anything. Left her to wonder why he'd said it with so much emotion throbbing behind the words.

It wasn't like him.

Last night, the fire department and a large gathering of neighbors had been all over the general vicinity of the house. If anyone other than the fire department had attempted to enter, it wouldn't have gone unnoticed. But tonight was a completely different story.

The neighborhood had reverted back to its peaceful state. Occasionally, the headlights of a car would slice through the darkness, but as the hours crept by, fewer and fewer vehicles passed the house. Fewer people to notice anything out of the ordinary.

Brian figured that Ben was counting on that.

He sat in the living room with the lights off, the smell of the extinguished fire all around him. He hardly noticed. He was listening for the sound of someone trying to come in.

A little after midnight he began to think this was a wild-goose chase, that Ben's only purpose was to scare Lila as an act of revenge because she'd gone on with her life. He debated calling it a night and just going home. After all, Lila was waiting for him.

And then he heard something. Not from within the house, but outside. The window he'd broken in order to get in last night made it easy to hear the sounds of the night.

Someone or something was out in the detached garage.

Any sleepiness he might have felt instantly evaporated. Brian took out his weapon and slowly made his way outside. The noise he'd heard continued. It sounded like a sledgehammer coming in contact with a hard substance.

Concrete?

Gun at the ready, Brian slowly approached the garage. A low light seeped out from beneath the door.

He was right. Someone was in there.

Chapter 16

Where was he?

Dropping the corner of the drape, Lila moved away from the window. At this rate, she would wear a path across the carpet from the living room sofa to the bay window. For the umpteenth time, she'd thought she heard Brian's car approaching.

Lila dashed back to the window. This time it was one of the neighbors down the block, coming home late.

Late.

It was past eleven and Brian was now officially more than just a little late. He was a lot late. For a fleeting moment she debated calling him on his cell, then abandoned that idea. She didn't want him thinking she needed her man to account for every moment spent out of her sight. She wasn't trying to keep him on a short leash. That wasn't her way.

Lila ran her hand along the back of her neck. Not one but all four of her children had shown up tonight with one vague excuse or another to check up on her. She appreciated it and while they were here, distracting her, that small, nagging feeling in the pit of her stomach faded. But now that she was alone, it was back. She'd been wrestling with her nerves for the past forty-five minutes, ever since Frank had gone home. Something was wrong.

When she and Brian had been partners, she'd learned to trust those feelings, to go with them. It was like having a sixth sense. She had to admit the alarm in her hadn't gone off in a long time, but now here it was, whispering in her ear, telling her that something was off.

She was letting her imagination run away with her. Ever since she'd begun to entertain the possibility that Ben wasn't dead.

Closing her eyes, she ran her hands up and down her arms, as if that would somehow help her shed this feeling. It wouldn't go.

Go to bed, she ordered herself. Who knew how long Brian would be gone and she did have work in the morning. She should be sleeping, not pacing and watching for cars.

Lila sighed. Who was she kidding? She couldn't sleep, not when she was keyed up like this. No way in hell was she going to resort to her old remedy and drink a glass of warm milk. Right about now she doubted if she would ever be able to face another glass of milk— warm or cold—again.

Okay, no milk. Then what?

Maybe she could read herself to sleep, Lila thought. That had worked more than once, even if the book she was reading was one of those exciting, edge-of-your-seat kind of thrillers. Two pages and she'd be gone. Three, tops.

Lila frowned. That sounded good, but the problem was, she had no books with her. But Brian did, she recalled suddenly. She knew for a fact that he had several shelves' worth of bestselling mysteries as well as a slew of technical books dealing with the latest advances in police procedures. She smiled to herself. Now there was something that was guaranteed to put her to sleep.

Feeling hopeful, trying her best to squelch the uneasy feeling, she made her way to Brian's den.

It was at the rear of the house. The door was open but the lights were off.

She peered in for a moment.

Next you're going to be afraid of monsters in the closet, she mocked herself.

After flipping on the light switch, she crossed to the shelves on the right. Brian kept his mysteries there, his nonfiction books on the shelves on the left. Between the two bookcases was his desk, a scarred, highly polished piece that had originally belonged to his grandfather. It was Brian's favorite piece of furniture. He'd told her that he could remember hiding under the desk as a boy, spinning scenarios of bravery in his head. He'd been thrilled when his grandfather had willed it to him.

Lila smiled. She could almost see Brian now, sitting on the black, swivel, high-back chair, poring over some case file—just like the one that was carelessly tossed on it now.

As she passed, Lila accidentally hit a corner of the file with her hip. The slender manila-colored file did a half turn and fell from the desk onto the floor. The two sheets that had been housed inside slipped out.

"Getting clumsy in your old age, Lila, my girl," she muttered under her breath. With a sigh, she bent down and picked up the folder and the sheets.

Neatly printed words across the top of the first sheet caught her attention. Instead of putting the sheets back into the folder, she began to read first one, then the other.

And when she was finished, she reread them. Twice.

It took several minutes for her heart to stop pounding so wildly in her chest. But that was only because the pounding had moved up to her ears.

There were no windows looking into the garage, no way for Brian to see in or get a heads-up as to where the intruder was in relation to the side door. He only had the sound of the sledgehammer to guide him.

Holding his breath, he waited for the next burst of noise, hoping there would be more.

He didn't have long to wait.

One hand on the doorknob, his gun ready in the other, Brian eased open the side door. As he'd hoped, the intruder wasn't close. Swinging the sledgehammer, the man was making contact with the rear wall.

Completing the swing, he broke through. The plasterboard beneath the thin veneer of concrete gave way. A gaping hole exposed a pocket of space. Approximately a foot beyond it was another wall.

Most likely the true wall, Brian thought.

Brian's eyes immediately shifted back to the intruder. He saw the man's profile.

Damn.

"So I was right." As he said it, the last of his disbelief slipped away. "You are still alive."

Startled, Ben spun around, surprise and anger stamped on his face.

Brian caught his breath. Even in the dim light, Lila's husband looked far more than merely three years older. His face was a mask of lines and leather. The malevolent expression in Ben's dark eyes bore into him. He was still clutching the sledgehammer.

"Put down the hammer," Brian ordered, his voice rumbling across the stillness.

Ben made no move to obey. Instead, for a moment, his face appeared to soften. As if Ben knew something about him that he didn't.

He nodded toward the hole he'd just made. "There's more than enough here," Ben told him. "You could be richer than your wildest dreams."

Brian wasn't even remotely tempted. Money had never meant that much to him. At most, it was a way to take care of his own.

"What makes a man rich isn't something you can stuff behind a wall, McIntyre."

Despite the gun, Ben sneered at him. "Don't give me that crap, Cavanaugh. That was the kind of stuff that Lila would spout." The laugh that escaped his lips was dark, threatening. "But then, I guess if you've been sleeping with her, it probably rubbed off." His thin lips spread out in a cold, nasty smile. "How about that, Cavanaugh? You finally got to sleep with my wife the way you wanted to all these years." He raised his chin in a pugnacious, silent challenge. "So, how's it feel? Good? Does she make you feel good?"

Brian had no intentions of dignifying the taunt with an answer. "Is this why you've been playing mind games with her?" he demanded, indicating the hole Ben had made. "To get her to leave so you could come and finally get the money you stashed there?" All this time, he thought, the money had been right under their noses. Who would have thought it?

Ben's eyes narrowed. "She was supposed to sell the damn house. She always said she'd sell it once the kids moved out. I even had Ri—someone come by and offer to buy it from her. Made her a damn good offer for the lousy place. But she said she wasn't selling. She always was perverse," he bit off.

The near slip had caught Brian's attention. So Ben was working with a partner. Who? He was going to have to ask Lila if she remembered the name of the person who'd approached her about buying the house.

"So when she wouldn't sell, you decided to burn it down instead and kill her in the process? What the hell happened to you, McIntyre?" Brian spat out. "You used to be a decent cop."

"Don't you judge me," Ben warned. "Don't you stand there like some high-and-mighty king and judge me. And no, damn it, I didn't try to burn it down. I wouldn't kill Lila. Rita did that. Rita and her damn jealousy because she thought I was still in love with Lila."

"Rita," Brian repeated the name. No image came to mind. "Is that your accomplice?"

A haughty look came into Ben's eyes. "I guess I can satisfy your curiosity, seeing as how one of us is not leaving here alive." His hands tightened around the sledgehammer. "Walker and I were double-crossed. Funny, right? The double agent was double-crossed. The drug cartel's man killed Walker, damn near killed me before I shot him. He was my height, close to my coloring. I figured I had to disappear because his pals would be after me. So I took his clothes and gave him mine. Gave him my wedding ring, too."

"And the teeth?"

"Smashed in as insurance. I figured you'd think I was tortured." That was exactly what they did think, Brian recalled. "Rita's the one who saved my life, gave me a place to stay while I healed. It took all this time before we were finally ready and I could get the money back." The angry frustration rose in his voice. "If she hadn't been so damn jealous of Lila, all this could have gone off without a hitch." He cursed the woman roundly. "The bitch almost ruined everything."

"Where is she now?" Brian asked, taking care not to have his back to the door.

Ben's eyes narrowed to slits. "She brought it on herself," was his answer.

He'd killed her, Brian thought. Maybe, in his own way, McIntyre still did love Lila. But that changed nothing.

"Put that hammer down," Brian ordered again. He cocked his weapon, aiming the barrel straight at Ben. "Now."

Ben smirked. "Whatever you say, 'Chief.'"

It happened so quickly that it only registered with Brian after the fact. One moment, Ben was carefully setting down the sledgehammer, resting it on its head while his fingers remained on the long shaft. The next moment a power sander Ben had snatched from the workbench to his left came flying at his head.

Stumbling back, trying to get out of the way, Brian had no time to react to the man who came sailing at him right behind the sander.

The air was knocked out of him as he fell backward. Ben was right over him, his legs on either side of his torso like a large, flesh-and-blood parenthesis.

Without missing a beat, Ben jerked the sander up from the floor. Holding it with both hands over Brian's head.

"Like I said, only one of us is leaving here alive." As he hefted the power tool over his head for maximum impact, his eyes on his enemy, Ben's face suddenly contorted in shock and pain. Still holding the sander, he stared down at the hole in his chest and the blood poring out of it. With supreme effort, he managed to look up, this time toward the doorway.

His lips twisted in an ironic smile. "You always could shoot better than me."

They were the last words he would ever utter. The next moment, as Brian rolled out of the way, Ben and the power sander he still clutched came crashing down to the floor.

Brian was on his feet in a minute, twisting around as he rose. Lila stood in the doorway, a plume of smoke drifting up from her service revolver. Her expression was stony.

He lost no time crossing to her. She felt rigid when he put his hand on her arm, moving the weapon's muzzle so that it pointed at the floor.

"Lila, what are you doing here?"

"Saving your life, it appears."

When he brought it up later, she had no recollection of saying that.

Like someone in a nightmare, she walked over to the prone body of her husband. His eyes seemed to stare at her.

Even though his face was now frozen in death, she leaned over to check for a pulse. There was none.

"And ending his," she whispered more to herself than to Brian.

She felt Brian's hands on her shoulders as he lifted her back up to her feet. Felt his warmth as he embraced her after taking her gun from her.

"I'm sorry," Brian told her softly.

She looked up at him, an enigmatic smile on her lips. "Sorry that I saved your life?"

He returned her smile, sensing all the unresolved issues that had to be bouncing around within her. But at least now, there would be closure. "No, sorry that you were the one who had to shoot him."

Everything was falling into place in her head. She let out a shaky breath. "Well, he did try to kill me first." Lila was surprised when Brian shook his head, negating her words.

"He said he didn't start the fire." He glanced back at the man's body and paused to bend down and shut Ben's eyes. According to him, someone named Rita did."

"Rita?" she repeated, stunned. "Rita Nunez?" she asked. It made sense now.

Brian couldn't help her there. "He didn't use a last name."

Lila was certain she was right. It had to be Rita Nunez. "Rita Nunez was the dispatch operator Ben was always flirting with. She quit abruptly right around the same time he was supposedly killed. Everyone thought it was because she couldn't handle his death. I guess we know better now, don't we?" Lila felt as if the air had been knocked out of her. "I should have realized something was up when she asked to buy my house."

"What?"

"Just before things got all weird with the phone calls and all, Rita turned up, said she'd been away. Made me an offer on the house because, according to her, she'd always liked the neighborhood. I directed her toward a house that was on sale on the next block. She thanked me and I never heard from her again." Lila banked down the emotions that threatened to overcome her and looked at Brian. Her eyes washed over him, looking for wounds or bruises. "Are you all right?"

He nodded. "Thanks to you." Ushering her aside, away from the body, he took out his cell phone. He needed to make a call, but first, he needed to find something out. "How *did* you happen to be here?"

"When you didn't come home, I started to have this uneasy feeling that something was wrong—like in the old days," she reminded him. "I knew I couldn't sleep, so I went into your den to see if there was anything that I could read." She couldn't quite keep the accusation out of her voice. "Funny thing happened on my way to the bookshelves—I accidentally knocked down the folder on your desk—the one with the DNA results in it." Her eyes narrowed. She'd trusted this man. Trusted him far more than she ever had her husband. Had she misplaced her trust, after all? "Why didn't you tell me?"

He'd tried to shield her and now he was going to pay for it. So be it. "I was going to."

"When?" she demanded.

"Soon." He wasn't going to apologize. Everything he'd done had been with her in mind. "You'd just been through a lot these last couple of days and I was afraid that this would be too much for you. The proverbial straw that would break you."

She was silent for a long moment, trying to deal with her disappointment, trying to find an excuse for his behavior. Had they gotten so out of touch that he didn't know her anymore?

"You didn't used to underestimate me, Brian."

Brian placed a call to the morgue for a wagon to come and collect Ben's body. When the man on the other end began to ask questions, Brian cut him short. This wasn't the time to go into details. Not until he got things cleared up on the home front.

Closing the phone, he put it away. Only then did he answer her comment. "I didn't used to love you as much as I do. That still doesn't explain how you came to be here."

He saw a hint of a smile curve her mouth. "Because

we think alike," she reminded him. "Once I knew Ben was alive, I figured he was trying to get rid of me so he could get his hands on whatever it was that he'd left here. And then I remembered the garage. It used to be his workshop, his domain. He'd never let us in, said he needed to be alone, to make things so that he could knock off some steam. After I thought he was dead, I couldn't make myself go in here, so I left everything the way it was."

She looked over toward the hole in the false wall. Ben had to have done all that before he'd gone into hiding. Damn, how could she have been so blind, so terribly naive?

"I guess he'd been planning to steal that money for a long time." Lila sighed. "It wasn't just a spontaneous thing, a temptation he'd encountered and couldn't turn his back on. He planned this."

Because he could see that hurt her, Brian said, "We'll probably never know."

But she had a different thought. "If we track down Rita, we might be able to get some answers and find out." How long had that been going on? she wondered. How long had she struggled to be faithful to Ben, only to have him conducting an affair right under her nose right up to the day he disappeared?

Brian shook his head. "From the way Ben talked, I don't think that's going to be possible." She eyed him quizzically. As much as he wanted to condemn McIntyre, the man had a few good qualities. "He sounded pretty angry that she'd tried to kill you in the fire. I think that Ben cared about you until the end."

"Not so's you'd notice. The milk was drugged," she reminded him. "Only my kids and Ben knew I drank a glass of milk before going to bed at night. But this does answer one question."

"What?"

"Why Duchess never barked when I thought some-one had gotten in the house. She knew Ben, she wouldn't have barked at him." She glanced over her shoulder at the body of the father of her children, her heart twisting in her chest. "Even though it hardly looked like him anymore," she added softly.

The sound of sirens were heard faintly in the back-ground. Lila shook her head, a half smile gracing her lips. "I think my neighbors are going to band together and petition for me to move away. I seem to attract sirens lately."

Brian slipped his arm around her. "I've got just the place for you."

He meant with him. Lila shook her head. "That's very nice of you, but I can't move in with you, Brian. What would my children say?" Then she did him one better. "What would your children say?"

Her protest didn't daunt him. "Probably something like, 'Hey, look, Mom and Dad are living together.' Or..." He reconsidered. "They might not say anything at all, considering that it's pretty common stuff to have a husband and wife living in the same house."

Lila stared at him. "Husband and wife," she echoed.

"Yes."

"You and me."

"That's who I had in mind."

Just so this was perfectly clear, she wanted him to spell it out for her. "You're asking me to marry you."

"Yes. For the second time," he reminded her. "I'd like that answer now."

He was pressing her because he thought it was the right thing to do, she thought. She wasn't going to have him proposing out of a sense of obligation. "Because I saved your life."

"Because if you married me," he corrected, "you'd be saving my life. Otherwise, I'm going to turn into one of those grumpy old men who lash out at everyone and forgets where they put their glasses."

It was really hard now not to grin. "You don't wear glasses."

He took the observation in stride. "I'm looking ahead into the future. And without you by my side," he told her seriously, "it looks pretty bleak."

Suddenly her heart felt very full. There was no longer any point in denying how she felt. She loved this man. "You always did have a way with an argument."

He grinned. "Then you'll marry me?"

Her eyes danced. "What do you think?" She brushed her lips against his.

"Yes?" he said hopefully. He'd learned long ago when it came to women to take nothing for granted.

"That's the word." She laughed as the sounds of the approaching sirens growing louder.

If she had anything else to say, it would have to wait. She'd always known it was hard to talk and kiss at the same time.

Epilogue

A wedding.

Andrew Cavanaugh smiled broadly to himself as myriad menus and plans ricocheted through his brain. It was a toss-up which he liked better as an excuse for a party, weddings or births. A birth meant a brand-new Cavanaugh had entered the world, but weddings, well, there was a soft spot in his heart for weddings. Weddings held the promise of the future. Of something grand and glorious just on the horizon.

Like more births.

There was no point in trying to debate the subject with himself. The truth was he loved any occasion that allowed him to gather his growing clan together. He loved cooking and he loved his family, not necessarily in that order, and this promised to yield the best of both worlds.

Brian and Lila belonged together, he told himself, just as he and Rose did.

Life was short and happiness was fleeting. In his opinion, no one should miss an opportunity to savor happiness.

And the nice thing was, he thought with a smile, Lila was bringing in new blood. Four more young people would be at the table and eventually, that would be eight and then more. Cavanaughs by marriage.

God, it was good to be alive, he thought, humming to himself.

He was just about to go upstairs in search of his favorite cookbook. As was the custom, the reception was going to be held in his backyard and he was determined to pull out all the stops to make it the most memorable of memorable events. Considering his previous triumphs, this was going to be a challenge.

Andrew had one foot on the stairs when he heard the doorbell. Rose was out, shopping. Once upon a time there'd be five other people around to get the door, but right now, there was only him.

The cookbook would keep, he thought, turning from the stairs.

The doorbell rang again. Maybe it as his imagination, but it sound more insistent this time. It couldn't be one of the kids because his two sons and three daughters still all had keys to the house.

"Hold your horses," he called. "I'm coming."

Reaching the front door, Andrew flipped the lock and opened it.

Not many things took Andrew Cavanaugh by surprise these days. He'd seen a great deal in his lifetime as a policeman and then as the police chief. But this, this really did take him by surprise.

He realized that he was staring.

If he hadn't been aware of what year it was, Andrew would have sworn that his brother—his dead brother—was standing on his doorstep.

Mike, looking the way he had in his early twenties.

On either side of the young man on his doorstep were two other people, another young man and a young woman. The latter made him think of his daughter, Rayne, before she ceased being such a handful. The former looked enough like the young man in the middle to be his brother.

"Can I help you?" he heard himself asking.

"Maybe," the young man in the middle replied. There was no hint of a smile, no attempt at a greeting. He was deadly somber as he said, "We're your brother Mike's bastards."

* * * * *

Don't miss Marie Ferrarella's next romance,
A DOCTOR'S SECRET,
available March 2008 from
Silhouette Romantic Suspense.

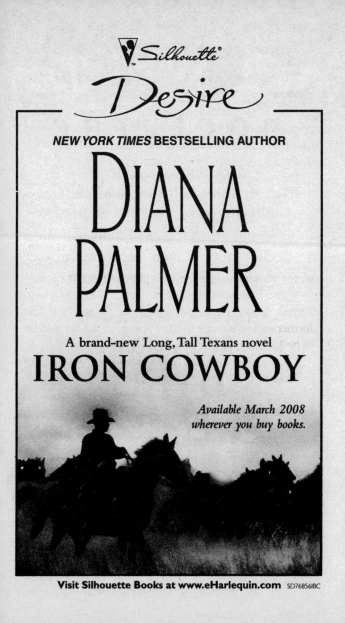

Silhouette®

Desire

NEW YORK TIMES BESTSELLING AUTHOR

DIANA PALMER

A brand-new Long, Tall Texans novel

IRON COWBOY

*Available March 2008
wherever you buy books.*

$1.**^{00} **OFF

The bestselling Lakeshore Chronicles continue with *Snowfall at Willow Lake*, a story of what comes after a woman survives an unspeakable horror and finds her way home, to healing and redemption and a new chance at happiness.

SUSAN WIGGS

NEW YORK TIMES BESTSELLING AUTHOR

SUSAN WIGGS

"Susan Wiggs's novels are beautiful, tender and wise."
—Luanne Rice

Snowfall at Willow Lake
The Lakeshore Chronicles

On sale February 2008!

SAVE $1.**^{00} off the purchase price of **SNOWFALL AT WILLOW LAKE by Susan Wiggs.

Offer valid from February 1, 2008, to April 30, 2008.
Redeemable at participating retail outlets. Limit one coupon per purchase.

5 2 6 0 8 1 6 8

5 65373 00076 2   (8100) 0 11463

MSW2493CPN

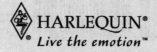

Bundles of Joy—
coming next month to Superromance

Experience the romance, excitement and joy with 6 heartwarming titles.

BABY, I'M YOURS #1476 by *Carrie Weaver*

ANOTHER MAN'S BABY
(The Tulanes of Tennessee)
#1477 by *Kay Stockham*

THE MARINE'S BABY (9 Months Later)
#1478 by *Rogenna Brewer*

BE MY BABIES (Twins)
#1479 by *Kathryn Shay*

THE DIAPER DIARIES (Suddenly a Parent)
#1480 by *Abby Gaines*

HAVING JUSTIN'S BABY (A Little Secret)
#1481 by *Pamela Bauer*

Exciting, Emotional and Unexpected!

Look for these Superromance titles in March 2008.
Available wherever books are sold.

Romantic

SUSPENSE

COMING NEXT MONTH

#1503 A DOCTOR'S SECRET—Marie Ferrarella
The Doctors Pulaski
Dr. Tania Pulaski vows never to get involved with a patient. Then Jess Steele enters her ER. Although he's strong and attractive, she hesitates taking things to the next level...until someone starts stalking her and she must trust the one man who can help her.

#1504 THE REBEL PRINCE—Nina Bruhns
Serenity Woodson knows the charismatic and sexy man who's been helping her aunt must be a con man. Then she learns the incredible truth—Carch Sunstryker is a prince from another planet, on a mission to Earth that may save his kingdom. Loving him would be insanity—but neither can resist the intense attraction that could destroy them both.

#1505 THE HEART OF A RENEGADE—Loreth Anne White
Shadow Soldiers
After Luke Stone fails to protect his wife and unborn child, he refuses to take on another bodyguard assignment. But when he becomes the only man who can protect foreign correspondent Jessica Chan from death, he faces the biggest challenge of his life...because being so close to Jessica threatens to break his defenses.

#1506 OPERATION: RESCUE—Anne Woodard
Derrick Marx will do anything to rescue his brother from the terrorists holding him captive, including kidnapping the reclusive botanist whose knowledge of the jungle is the key to his success. Against her will, Elizabeth Bradshaw leads Derrick through the jungle, but quickly find the forced intimacy is more dangerous than the terrorists themselves.

SRSCNM0208